D1176537

Also by Phyllis Wachob

Teachers Abroad Mysteries

#1 Revolution Revenge
#2 Oasis Assassin
#3 Turkish Delight Gone Sour
#4 Singapore Fling

Kern Kapers Mysteries

#1 Body in the Orchard

Body
in the
Orchard

Phyllis Wachob

Dedication

This novel is dedicated to all those who have a love/hate relationship with their hometown.

Acknowledgements

Although the general impression is that writers struggle alone, those of us who write know this is not the case. Family gives us time and space to grapple with the story, friends encourage us by asking how it goes, critique groups encourage us by giving honest feedback, designers and photographers help us feed on our collective creativity, and proofreaders keep us honest and true to our craft. So, thanks to my Mom, my friends, my Writers of Kern critique group members, my cover designer Doug Thompson, my photographer Francisco Montesinos, my friend Jennette Green who helped with formatting, my proofreader Jackson Huston and my webpage designer Keith Silvas. A special thank you goes to all my fellow members of the Writers of Kern, who keep the encouragement coming.

Preface

Although some of the places in this novel are real, for example Trout's, Woolgrowers, and Bill Lee's, most are fictional. The real places of Bakersfield and Kern County are easily found in histories, maps, guides and on the web. However, Darrell Pitt's office, the unnamed orchard in Delano and the Harger house in Tehachapi are fictional. In its essence, this is a work of fiction. Names, characters, places and incidents are either the product of the author's imagination or are used fictitiously, and any resemblance to actual persons, living or dead, businesses or establishments, events or locales is coincidental.

Cast of Characters

Vermilion Blew: retired school librarian and teacher

Frankie Monroe: Very's fiancé

Joey Sanchez: Very's best friend

Darrell Pitts: Private Investigator

Sunny Monroe: Frankie's mother

Marty Monroe: Frankie's sister

Danny Harger: friend of Frankie's

Ruth 'Babe' Harger: Danny's wife

Cassandra Harger: Danny's daughter

Deputy Sanchez: Joey's husband

Stanley 'Q-Ball' Leon: Danny's friend

Glenn 'Curly' Wilson: Danny's friend

Father Sullivan: Danny's high school classmate

Chapter One: A Body in the Orchard

"Body Found in Orchard" read the headline. Very shook the paper and let her eyes travel to the article in the lower right-hand corner of page two. So what else was new? Bodies were found all the time in the orchards in Bakersfield. Was this one new, lying on top of the newly-fallen leaves, or was it old, buried beneath the cement-hard clay soil? Killed there? Or more likely, dumped there as a convenient alternative to someone's backyard.

Vermilion Blew looked at her own backyard, dominated by a huge sycamore, now beginning to drop its large brown leaves into the blue waters of the small backyard pool. She heard the hum of the pool pump and gritted her teeth yet another time. Dollars, draining from her checking account, to enrich the greedy electric company and the pool maintenance crew. The slow leak that defied the experts and threatened to get her in trouble with the water board in the era of drought. And because the fall weather had arrived, it was too cold to swim in.

She glanced at the headline again. Should she bother to read the article? She glimpsed at the clock over the sink. 8:30. She smiled and sighed with deep satisfaction. No more early morning library openings, no more classes with bored teenagers, no more meetings with 'diarrhea mouth' colleagues. Retirement suited her. She looked more closely at the article.

The teacher who had read student essays for over 30 years could not help the analysis. Was the article short, to the point? Did it answer the crucial questions? Where? On the west side of the valley, where new orchards had sprouted in the last 35 years, taking over the cotton fields with a more lucrative crop. Well, at least the almond blooms in February were a distraction and an alternative to wild flower displays in the years of drought. And the almonds and pistachios brought in money and a few jobs for the farm workers.

Did it say when? Woops, doesn't say. Presumably in the last few days. And an old body, because there was no name, yet. Gender? Ninety percent or more were male, so let's say it fits the profile and it was a man. Buried? Yep. So, how was it found? Who found it? Why? Very read the next three paragraphs, which filled in the details.

Then the cat meowed to be let out. Very stood and slid open the back window, waited for the cat to exit and then she stepped out into the cool morning. The sun shone brightly, reflecting off the pool and deep cool shadows lured the cat to explore their depths. Bakersfield had marvelous weather, for six weeks every fall and six weeks every spring. But the summers were viciously hot, the winters were cold and gloomy and it was only the shoulder seasons that tempted an outdoor lifestyle. Despite this, Bakersfieldians pretended they could run, play football and bicycle all year round. And died proving it. Maybe the body was one of those athletes that had died trying to prove a point?

Very went back to the paper. She read the funnies, glanced at the advice columns, checked the opinion page. Conservative did not adequately describe the letters to the editor, which often fell far off the edge of modern reason. The obituaries. Her mother always read them, usually first thing. Very looked across the table at the empty chair. Wasn't it time to get rid of it; put it elsewhere? Her mother's body was safely in the ground, the headstone reminding all when she was born and when she died. Couldn't she put away the chair? She hadn't been able to bring herself to sit in it, even when visitors came and sat in her chair. So why not put it in the garage, give it to Goodwill, take it to the dump, or at least take it away from the spot at the table where her mother had always sat? Very sprang up and violently grabbed the chair, hauling it on squeaking, protesting wheels into the spacious bedroom at the back of the house. She pushed it up against the king-sized bed that dominated the room. Very backed out and slammed the door, turning her back to the room that still smelled of sickness, unwashed sheets and her mother. She inhaled and let her breath out slowly, pushing the wind from her lungs until there was nothing left. Then she sucked in life-giving air and strode back to the kitchen table. She gave the table a shove towards the wall, erasing the space where the chair had been and giving her more room on 'her' side of the table. She picked up her coffee cup and the paper and went through the sliding glass door to the patio.

She eased herself into one of the rocking chairs just now edging into the sun. She stretched her long legs in front of her and sighed. Raking her fingers through her short brown and gray hair she huffed over her actions with the chair. Did this mean she was ready to push her mother and all those possessions out of her space? Make a life and a journey of her own? Finally? At one point, an uncle told her she was a 'big girl now' and laughed. She had always been a big girl, tall, broad shouldered, top heavy and burdened with average looks. Her uncle had been deliberately cruel and she had cringed. A big girl, get a life. She turned to the paper.

But what about that body? She flipped through the pages again until she found the article.

"Investigators have reported that the body was found when the orchard was being dismantled in preparation for new trees. 'This is done every 30 or so years. The trees just get too old and don't produce as much. Then we have to tear them all out and plant new ones,' explained the orchard owner. The police have speculated that the body was buried at that time. 'The whole place would have been torn up then. We bring in heavy equipment to dig the holes for new trees and no one would have noticed disturbances in the soil.' Police think that the body of a man was buried there as it was convenient at the time.

"They believe it is the body of a man as the body was dressed in men's clothes, including a sports coat. There is no identification on the body or any watches, jewelry or other personal possessions. However, the investigators said a partially destroyed ticket was in the pocket.

One clue to the date of the body is on the ticket. Investigators believe it may be from the Nile Theater as 'ile' can clearly be read. A date of 4/20/7 can be seen as well. The County Sheriff's Department is asking that anyone who has any knowledge or evidence concerning this person contact them."

Very read the last paragraph three times. At the end of the third time, her heart began to race and thump in her chest, her breathing came short and shallow. A loud buzz echoed in her brain. She put her head down and gulped air, trying to right the balance in her head and heart.

She went back to the article. The Nile Theater, Friday night, Good Friday, the day before her wedding. She would never forget the day. It was a John Wayne movie, not what she would have chosen, but he wanted to go. The theater was full and they had sat down next to other people. She remembered the conversing, but not the details of the conversation with the guy sitting next to him. The lights went down, the coming attractions started, but still the two young men whispered. She finally dug him in the ribs. "Shush," she had said. She didn't follow the movie, but went over the schedule for the next day's events.

Very looked at the sycamore tree. It had been a sturdy little tree then; green shoots and tiny leaves would have made a natural background for the white flowers and white and pink ribbons. Everything was ready when five o'clock came, but the groom didn't come. His mother and sister arrived and were surprised that he wasn't already there. Phone calls were made and at seven they all went home.

She would never forget that Friday night. It was the last time she ever saw or heard from Frankie Monroe.

Now, the buzz came back, louder and more insistent. Very tried to breathe slowly and deeply, but the roar kept getting louder and louder, drowning out her efforts to control the fog. Blackness descended and she slowly slipped out of her chair and gently rolled onto the patio bricks in a profound faint.

Chapter Two: The Suitcase

Very stood in front of the closet. The door was a sliding door to a very small closet. The makers of the 1950's era house wanted a modern sliding door, but there wasn't really enough room for a full-sized closet, hence this miniature opening. This was the third bedroom of the house and had only ever been used as a guest room. A single bed was shoved against one wall, boxes lined a second wall, stacked as high as the girls had dared, and the miniature closet took up the fourth wall. A row of high windows, just enough to let in some light, hovered above the bed. An old poster of the Golden Gate Bridge still clung to the wall where some energetic teenager longing for blue skies and ocean had taped it. The bed held a set of clean sheets on top of the faded bedspread. If you wanted to sleep on clean sheets, you needed to make the bed yourself – that had always been the rule in this house. The walls had been painted pale yellow and although they had not faded, they might have done and no one would be the wiser. A sad little room, musty-smelling and neglected. The last person to sleep here was her sister, when their mother lay dying in the master bedroom. Sissy had stayed in a hotel at the funeral and hadn't been back since. Well, Sissy could sleep in the old woman's bed when she came back, if she wanted to sleep in this house.

Even though she knew exactly where she had placed the suitcase, she pretended to push aside old dresses with an air of bewilderment. Who wore dresses these days? She reached into the farthest corner of the closet and touched the hard-sided suitcase. A weekend bag, it was called, just enough for a few changes of clothes and a swimsuit. She struggled to find the handle and when she did, she struggled to pull it out; stacks of old shoes and boxes of papers lay in its path out of the closet. "Oomph," Very said as the case popped out of the detritus.

Very took the case and heaved it easily onto the bed, and sat down beside it. She touched the fading, yellow, crinkly, hard, man-made material that was all the rage when she got it for her first real trip out of town at age 15. Her dad bought it for her. It was on sale, no choice of color, but still, new and modern. She had taken it to college and carried it on all the important weekend jaunts she had taken to the City and Berkeley. Even when her friends had transitioned to backpacks and duffel bags, she had lovingly packed her underwear, shoes in little bags, pants, shirts, blouses all folded to fit on one side. Dresses, even though they were 'granny dresses' or hippie dresses, were folded and placed on the upper side with a yellow strap to keep them neat when the suitcase was tipped up.

Very found the two sliding metal tabs and tried to open them. Stuck or locked? Very looked closely and saw flakes of rust around the keyholes and along the edge of the mechanism. She leveraged her forefinger under the edge and pushed; the lock squeaked and opened. Good, if this side was unlocked, so was the other. It just needed some force. The other side resisted until she retrieved an old rusty knife from the ancient and cheap everyday cutlery set. She pushed, nudged, and finally spit on it, loosening bits of the rust. It opened with a 'whack' and years of air whooshed into the interior.

Even though Very had packed it, she had few memories of doing so. The dark days following the aborted wedding were all a blur. They represented the lowest point in her life and not one that she thought she ever wanted to bring up again. She packed these things and said to herself that she would never look at them again. That was what she remembered. And that she had placed the suitcase, now outdated, into the farthest corner of this neglected closet. She had buried it.

Now she would dig it up. The suitcase opened into two halves. One half contained what appeared to be an old sheet, firmly held down by the ancient straps. She knew what it was. Leave it for the moment. The other half of the suitcase contained things other than clothes. The straps had broken on this side and the contents threatened to spill out onto the floor. Very grabbed the red padded book that was on top before it slid out. Her hands shaking, she opened it. The front page was blank. Why? What went on the first page of a wedding album? She turned to the second page. An envelope lay there, not stuck shut. Inside was a photocopied invitation to the casual wedding that was to take place. She had taken them to the shop that did proper wedding invitations but these were photocopies. It was a simple invitation. They were printed on one sheet and she had cut them apart with a pair of scissors to make two invitations. The envelopes were chosen to match the paper, which they did, badly. But at least they were invitations to a wedding that was to take place; not an after the fact, 'they eloped' kind of happening. She had been very clever, hadn't she, saving money on something that would be looked at twice, at most, and then thrown away. Why not save money for other things in life? This one had not been addressed to anyone, so maybe it was a left-over invitation, or one for the wedding album. She had hand delivered a few of them. One to Frankie's mother and sister, who lived not far, and another to her cousin on the other side of town. She read the invitation, from her parents, announcing and inviting guests to the wedding. It was melancholy to read about dead people, who had been so alive then, 37 years ago.

Very turned the page and touched the photos that lay between the pages. They had been taken the day of the wedding in the morning and had been done as a '2-hour print' and so were ready for the album, even before the wedding. She gritted her teeth as she touched them. There were 24 in all. The color had not faded; they could have just come from the photo finishing station at the local drug store. They seemed so forlorn now, little square reminders of a ceremony all prepared that never took place. The first page held the two photos that would have been the first glimpse that guests would have had of the backyard. The sycamore tree held tiny green buds and Sissy had tied ribbons on some of the branches, so it looked as if it were in flower with cheap pink and white ribbons tied in childish bows. Tables and chairs, a variety of borrowed ones and some that her parents owned, were set up in the patio and on bits of the lawn. Pink fabric covered them and vases with a tiny bunch of flowers sat on each table. Pink and white bows perched near the vases, giving it all a festive air. Obviously, pink and white were the colors for the wedding, but they had never been colors she had favored. Who had decided that 'pink' would be 'the color'? She shook her head. It had not been her choice.

The following pages held photos of the simple cake, a round pink and white confection of pink icing flowers and swirled white cream topping. What had the inside been? She would have favored carrot cake, but she couldn't remember what had been chosen. Maybe there was a receipt left here? Another photo was of Very's parents and Sissy, then one of Sissy by herself, dressed in her pink frothy dress as a bridesmaid, or was it a flower girl? Her best friend Joey appeared in one. Very hadn't dressed yet, but held a bouquet, the one that she was supposed to carry. It was small, tasteful and obviously inexpensive. Pink and white. It had come in a box; white, square and with a plastic top to see what was inside. She had not thrown it to the next bride-to-be.

Very looked at the other photos, including one of her in her wedding dress that morning. She paused and looked carefully. She had no make-up on and her hair flew around her shoulders, not yet 'fixed'. Someone had told her to check one last time that the dress was ready and to try it on. She had done as asked and Sissy, or was it Joey, snapped this casual photo. The only one of Very in her wedding dress. She looked at the now faded sheet, held tightly by the yellow (same color as the suitcase) straps. Could she stand to look at it? Would all these years have erased the pain of that day? Could she cope with the one most important remaining symbol of that day?

Flipping through the remaining photos, she noted that they had all been taken early in the day; the sun slanted into the yard leaving morning shadows. Someone, Joey maybe, had taken the film to the drug store and had it on hand just as she was getting into her dress in preparation for the ceremony that never happened. By the time she reached a quarter of the way through the album, she had run out of photos. Tucked into the next page was a handwritten list of invitees. Very's side of the family and her high school friends predominated the list. With an uneasy niggle at the back of her neck, she looked for the list of Frankie's family and friends. There was only one, his mother and sister. They were listed together with an address, not far from Very's address, but a neighborhood away. There was also a telephone number with the first two digits, not in numerical form, but in alphabetical format. How long ago was that style abandoned? A small yellowed clipping from the newspaper showed her senior high school photo along with a short article about the engagement. Date of wedding, age of bride and groom, daughter and son of. Everyone had one printed in the local paper. Even if you eloped or married out of town, it was still de rigueur to have the bride's photo and short article in the page that contained the rest of the county's engagement and wedding announcements. It wasn't the custom any longer. All was revealed on Facebook or some other online list. How does a mother cut out and preserve the announcement if it is only on Facebook? A quick flip through the rest of the album revealed a book of empty pages, waiting for photos and keepsakes. But there was no more.

Putting aside the album, Very sifted through the contents remaining in this half of the suitcase: a preliminary list of positive RSVP's, three pink and white bows that had decorated a table or tree, and a browned box with a plastic inset cover. Carefully, she removed and opened it. Her bouquet, browned and shriveled like a mummified apple. The small bow at the base of the bouquet was the only bright color, as if it was the only part that had wanted to survive and be opened 37 years later. How had this gotten into the suitcase? Her mother must have gathered it up and placed it back into the box;

sneaking it in when she was distracted. She knew nothing about how it arrived here. Also, there was a map of the backyard. Sissy's handwriting. Tables were indicated; chairs were drawn with names in a childish hand. "Mom, Dad, me, Joey, BRIDE and GROOM."

Gently undoing the clasps that held the sheet-wrapped wedding dress, Very pulled the package out. The sheet, browned in some places, yellow streaked in others, fell away from the frothy contents. The tulle overskirt filled and gently lifted itself, as if some inner life had waited to once again reveal its elegance after the confinement of years. Very stood and pulled it out to its full length. A smile tugged at her lips at the memory. Her mother had taken her to the French Shop. Not that the French Shop dealt in wedding gowns, they certainly didn't. But they did have a range of long gowns for proms and bridesmaids' dresses. The two had been in a hurry, needed a suitable dress that day or very soon. Her mother told Very that she would buy whatever she wanted. She had mentally discarded the idea of the ideal bride's dress of 1955 like the one her bride dolly had. She had only wished for it to be pretty, to have it fit well, to be worthy of the occasion of the small backyard wedding. The dress was white with a wide pink bow at the gathered waist. There was a lacy top to the bodice and the tulle overskirt was of the faintest pink. And it was 'tea length', not the fashion in 1973; indeed, it was 'retro' in so many ways. It was the ideal bride's dress of 1955. But the fit was right, not an easy thing with her height and angular shoulders, the lace at the neckline was elegant and she looked very, very good in it. It needed no alterations. It was ready to take home. Now, the pink bow was slightly bent in two places, but the sheet had preserved the dress and the overskirt in perfect condition. Very's lower lip quivered, until she bit down hard on it.

Her mother's comment when Very was packing the suitcase a week after the disastrous day came unbidden.

"Well," her mother had suggested, "you can always keep it and wear it on some other occasions. It would look nice going to the symphony or…"

Very had been startled at the insensitive implication. "How cruel of you!" Very had bitten back. "How can you even think of me wearing this again?"

Her mother had looked crushed. "I was only trying to help. You know, in my day we had to think of money and reusing everything. After all, I am a Daughter of the Depression."

Very tossed the dress aside and looked again at the suitcase. At the bottom of the suitcase was a photo, the only one that she had of the two of them. It was a large one, five by seven, but still amateur in composition and focus. They sat side by side, casual sweaters enveloped their shoulders and big grins lit their faces. Her dad had snapped the photo the day they had told her parents they were getting married. It was the 'engagement' photo, so she had it enlarged. She had hoped to put it in a frame on a mantelpiece along with a triumphant wedding photo. She looked at it with mature eyes.

God, he was good-looking! Dark hair, curly to the brink of being unruly. A wide forehead, deep set dark gray eyes, not black, not brown, with a hint of amber streaks in them. His even teeth were brilliant white, like an advertisement for a toothpaste or a high-class dental clinic. His smile was genuine, intimate, drawing the viewer inside to a heart happy with the occasion. This was just a few weeks before he left her. How could he have been so happy that day, and so angry or disappointed or frightened or overwhelmed or some other deeply-felt emotion that he had left just a few weeks later?

Maybe it was not because he wanted to leave, but some other reason? Such as being murdered and buried in an orchard.

Chapter Three: Call to the Sheriff

Finding the number was easy, it was speaking to the operator that was difficult. It wasn't an emergency, so Very felt hesitant to sound urgent. She felt the urgency, but hoped she had hidden the quaver in her voice and catch on the word 'body'. She was connected to Detective Williams.

"This is in relation to the body found in the orchard," she began hesitantly. "I think, maybe, that is, I think I know who it is."

She heard the scrapes and squeaks of a chair and then a commanding voice, "Yes, tell me what you know."

"I think maybe it's my fiancé, or was. That's because of the ticket in the pocket. We went to the movie and that was the last time I saw him." Very went quiet, waiting for questions.

"And…" prompted Detective Williams.

"He disappeared."

"Do you have any evidence, any way we can verify who the remains belong to? Things like dental records, clothes, photos and so forth."

"Yes, some." She suddenly felt silly. She didn't have any of that except a photo. It all seemed so implausible now.

"Why don't you come down here to our office and we can look into it," Detective Williams said.

"Now?"

"Why not? Bring what you have. I'll be waiting for you." He hung up.

Very looked at her phone and tried to digest what had been said. Obviously, she should go to the Sheriff's office, but wasn't this a long shot? Was he being rude and abrupt, or just businesslike? Did she have anything else but his photo? She dug into the suitcase again and found nothing else that was connected with the long-lost groom. She found a used envelope in the kitchen drawer and put the photo in it.

She had never visited the Sheriff's Department, but she knew where it was, out by the airport. All the other offices connected with the city and county, the courts and so forth, were downtown, where they had been since the founding of the city. The 52 earthquake had meant rebuilding and reshuffling, but they all still sat along Truxtun Avenue; multistory buildings advertising their importance in ruling and running the place. But the Sheriff's office had been moved to a bigger space, removed from the action. She couldn't remember why.

Very guided her car carefully to the one-story building on Norris Road. She parked in the shady parking lot and sat in her car. As she sat, a fog once again descended on her brain. She shook her head and took a deep breath. Her heart began to beat noisily in her chest. Very closed her eyes and commanded quiet in her head, and heart. When she felt composed, she entered the building. Security check, check in at the reception desk, take a seat. All these routine things slid past her easily. She sat in the waiting room chair, her ankles crossed, clutching her purse and envelope and watched the room.

An extended family sat together. Morose. Scared. A woman, her hair needing a shampoo and comb, sat squirming in a corner. A child sat on the floor at her feet. When the child whimpered, she leaned down and lifted him by an arm, as the great apes lift their youngsters. She settled him on her lap, pulled clothes from a bag and proceeded to dress the baby. Silent, both of them. Two men, father and son, or brothers, certainly belonging to the same family, sat chatting in low voices. They wore jeans, tee-shirts and day-old stubble clung to their faces. Bakersfieldians.

Soon Detective Williams called her and they went behind the door to a small private room. When they were seated, he asked, "May I tape record this?"

Very look startled.

"It saves time, and it means that I can be more accurate," he said peevishly.

"Of course, of course." She wasn't being judged or on trial. She had come to be helpful, so why should she hesitate? "Yes, by all means."

"Thanks," he clicked on a small recorder. He started by indicating the date, the place and who was present. "Now, tell me."

Very tried to be logical, accurate and told the story from the beginning of reading the paper that morning. "The ticket is from the Nile Theater, right? Well, I went to the movies that night with Frankie Monroe. It was a John Wayne western. I didn't really want to go, since we had our wedding the next day and I was really busy. We came home afterwards, he dropped me off at my house and I thought he went to stay with his mother, at her house not far away. But the next day, he wasn't anywhere. His mother and sister came to the wedding, at our house, and they thought he had come by himself. They hadn't seen him, didn't know where he was. And that was that."

"April 20, 1973, a Friday. That was the last time you saw or heard from him; what was his name?"

"Francis, I think. Maybe Franklin or Frank but everyone always called him Frankie. His last name is, was, is Monroe. I don't know his middle name."

"Birth date?"

"1948. I don't know the month and day, May maybe. It would have been on the license, but I don't have that. Frankie kept it. He said he would bring it to the wedding."

"Address?"

"Last known address?" Very referred to the list of the invited guests that she had shoved into her purse along with the photo. "Here," she pointed to the last name on the short list.

"This is the whole guest list? Hmm, small wedding."

"It was a small wedding, just family and a few friends. In my parents' back yard."

"So, what time was it you noticed he was missing? Just at the wedding?"

"I suppose we could say 5pm on April 21. But no one remembered seeing him that day."

"Were there any phone calls? When was the last time that he was known to be alive and well, that is?"

"As far as I can remember, it was a very confusing time, you understand, it was the evening of the movie. I might have been the last one to see him, that we know of."

"Missing person's report? When was that filed?" Detective Williams asked.

"I don't know. I don't think there was one. I didn't file it. Remember, he was only a fiancé, and he didn't show up to the wedding, so I wasn't related to him. It would have been his mother's job, I suppose."

"And you don't know if she ever filed a missing person's report?"

"No, I don't know. I wasn't in any condition to know or remember anything." Very sat back in the chair and took a deep breath. This was the first time she had spoken about Frankie and the wedding to anyone for many, many years. She had refused to speak to her mother about it. Sissy wasn't one for digging in the past. Her friend Joey had listened enough to the wails, the lamentations, the curses on the heads of all men, particularly Frankie Monroe, and no longer had ears for any of it.

"You see, Frankie's mom said that it wasn't a real shock. That the men in her family did things like that. I think her exact words were, "Useless man, just like his father." Because Frankie's father had left them, he grew up without a father. So, I believe that Frankie's mother had just thought that the apple hadn't fallen far from the tree and it was just like Frankie to run. And so, I thought he had jilted me. I was angry, humiliated, really, really upset and besides, I left town."

"And you heard nothing more? No phone calls, letters? What about his mother?"

"As far as I know, they heard nothing either. I think they would have let me know. I parted on good terms with them. I would have wanted to know, no matter what. I think they knew that, I hope they did. But now…?

"The man in the orchard was buried. You don't bury yourself and you don't bury random bodies that die unexpectedly in orchards, or anywhere else. We are treating this as a homicide." Detective Williams sighed. "We are trying to identify the man. Thanks for your help. I must admit that this looks as if we might be able to say that it is Frankie Monroe. But a theater ticket isn't enough. Do you have anything else?"

"Oh, a photo." Very took the photo from her purse. She held it out tentatively to the detective. "Taken about the end of March of that year."

The detective took a small camera and shot a photo of it. "Don't lose this. We may need it later. Do you have the negative?"

Very looked at the detective. "Probably. I have everything that ever came into that house. Nothing ever got thrown away. Nothing. Certainly not a negative or a photo. But where, I cannot tell you."

"And you haven't got anything that we could get DNA from? Not that we could afford to do a DNA analysis. Dental records? Or even the name of a dentist?"

"No, but his mother might have something. I don't know where she is living now, or even if she's still alive. Probably not alive anymore. He had a sister, Marty, Martha Monroe. But she has undoubtedly married and moved on. I guess that's all I have."

"We can check to see if there was a missing person's report. Frankly, it sounds like his mother didn't bother."

"It isn't as if I didn't really care. I did care about him. But I left town. I had a kind of nervous breakdown and I couldn't concentrate on things like missing person reports. I couldn't cope with anything. There was too much, too many things all at once." Very felt tears rise in her eyes.

"Wow, he must have been some guy! I can see being mad at him, but you seem like a very together sort of person. A nervous breakdown, that's a big reaction." The detective looked at Very with sad eyes, trying to convey his understanding and sympathy.

"It wasn't him. It was the miscarriage. Jilted at the altar and then... My poor lost baby."

Chapter Four: A Talk with Joey

Joann Sanchez was Very's very best, oldest friend. Well, Joey wasn't really her oldest friend, but she had been her friend in the worst of times, and had never deserted her in times of hardship, so it was to Joey that she turned. Very sat in her car in the Sheriff's parking lot and texted Joey, 'Can you talk now?' Very knew that Joey was a busy person. She had a husband, three sons, two daughters-in-law and one serious girlfriend-in-waiting. She had three grandchildren so far and was hoping for more. Although Joey was retired, her time was NOT her own. The reply was a quick, 'Sure.'

'I'm on my way.' Very backed out carefully, knowing it would not do to have an accident in the parking lot of the Sheriff's Office. She turned up the radio as she pulled out of the lot. It was a short drive to Joey's house. Although she still lived 'north of the river', it was in a classier part of town, just off Olive Drive.

As she drove, Very returned to her 'fuzzy' headedness from the morning. Twice today, once when she read the paper and another time talking with the detective. What could have caused it? It was as if her body had an allergic reaction to the news or the name or the situation. What could you expect with a shock like she had had that morning?

Joey had the door open before Very could punch the doorbell. "Come in. What's up?"

Very looked at Joey's attire. Yoga pants stretched across a toned, but not small derriere, a tight cap-sleeve tee-shirt held together a sagging bosom; flip-flops adorned with rhinestones sparkled on feet with purple nail polish; a plastic clip held only half of the full head of gray-streaked hair and a lurid shade of pink lipstick shone on Joey's full lips. Very shook her head, "Joey, yoga pants, really?"

"I don't go to the store in them! But they are comfortable, you should try them. Soda water, coffee, something stronger?"

"Coffee, I need some oomph about now. Or no, maybe some iced tea, it's getting warm. Let's sit outside." Very headed for the sliding glass door that led to the small backyard. It held a patio with a barbeque station, a small three-stroke pool and a corner of roses, still putting out vibrant blooms.

Very levered herself down onto a lounge chair with her feet in the sun, let her shoulders sag as she emptied her lungs, refilling them with the calmness of Joey's backyard.

"Okay, once more, what's up?" Joey demanded.

"Did you see the paper today, 'Body Found in Orchard'?"

"I guess I saw it, so what? What's unusual about that? Probably two a year, for the last umpteen years."

"What is unusual is the ticket in the pocket. They found a ticket in the pocket from the Nile Theater for April

20, 1973." Very let the information hang in the air, waiting for Joey to remember the date.

"So?"

"So, April 22 that year was Easter and the day before, Saturday, was supposed to be my wedding day. I went to the movies with the man in question on Friday April 20 at the Nile Theater."

"And you never saw him again!"

"Ah, the penny drops. They don't have any other identification, someone obviously went through his pockets before he was buried there. But Joey, what if it is Frankie Monroe?"

"Jilted at the altar, or the backyard pool, and then he turns up dead, how many years later?"

"Thirty-seven. I've just come from the Sheriff's office. I didn't have anything else to show them but the one photo. They asked if I had filed a missing person's report."

"The last thing on your mind at the time, girl."

"I hadn't thought about him in years, really thought about it all. I tried to tell the detective why I didn't pursue his disappearance. I mumbled something about his mother saying that he was just like his father, running away from responsibility. But what I should have said was the bald truth. My fiancé jilted me, my baby died and I went crazy."

"Oh no, Very. You had had a huge blow and you managed to get it together. I couldn't have done what you did. You are a survivor."

Very sat quietly and tried to rethink what had happened just in the last few hours. She had put Frankie and the past behind her, only to have a dead body become unburied and threaten to upset her life.

"I did it all so badly. I thought that having the wedding was the right thing. Hasn't it been that way for thousands of years? Someone told me that in some parts of Asia, it is a sign of good luck to be pregnant when you get married. After all, it shows fecundity and new life, a productive marriage. So why do we get so squeamish? My grandmother, my mother, they were pregnant too. It's just that I thought he had left me; that he had gotten cold feet and ran away. After all, Sunny Monroe told me that. But what if he didn't show up because he was murdered? All these years, I have thought so badly of him. I hated him, I cursed him, he was the devil incarnate, no one could have been worse than Frankie Monroe who not only left his bride, but his unborn child. What kind of loser does that?

"Now, I need to rethink everything. I thought I knew him and when he didn't show up, my first thought was a flat tire or his car broke down again or something like that. Oh God, not murder. I gave up too easily; I never tried to find him. After all, he was going to be my husband. Didn't I have any feelings for him? Didn't I love him?"

Joey jumped in, "Don't go there, Very. You've spent 37 years being disappointed and hating him. How can you tell if you loved him, or still love him? You only knew him for a few months that you could have said that you loved him, but you have lived with someone you hated for years and years."

"I fell apart back then. I just ran away, I disintegrated, I became a formless blob. I should have been proactive, looked for him, tried to save my baby. I know it was my fault that I had that miscarriage. I became too upset, I had so much anger and hate that I forced that child out of my system. What a terrible mother I was!"

"No, no, Very. You were in a delicate position, it could have happened to anyone, in fact it does. Do you know how many miscarriages there are? You had a blow, a hammer blow and you recovered. Two things in one week, and you survived. I couldn't have done that. No, Very, you are a survivor!"

"Lyrics to a bad song, not the reality."

"Wow, look how fast you got into Library School? Hey, no one else gets such late approval. And you never missed a class, never missed a single opportunity to make it all good again. And you came back here, so quickly, with a job, right out of your MA program. No, Very, you did a WONDERFUL JOB of picking yourself up and making a life."

"Then how come I never married? How come I didn't have a husband and children and a normal life?" Very's face burned with anger and frustration, pent up for years.

"Ah, that's another story, and you know it."

"And how do you know that? How do you know what's gone on in my head, making me do this or that, or not doing what I should be doing?"

Joey stood, hands on hips. "Vermilion Blew, you have had every day to make choices. A single event, even as terrible as being jilted or having a miscarriage, cannot change the day to day decisions that we make. YOU have made decisions, and don't blame them on Frankie Monroe or Mother Nature. If I remember, Frankie was the first real boyfriend you ever had, huh? And why didn't you hook up with anyone else before then? Were you so ugly, so fat, so antisocial, so, so, so… uninterested? NO. What changed? Nothing much, you remained yourself. Always! But, and this is a random thought, maybe Frankie really was the only one? The true love of your life?"

Very looked up at Joey. She whispered, "Maybe he was. I don't really remember what I felt, except the hurt and anger. Perhaps I have done him, and me, a terrible injustice."

They sat quietly for a few minutes listening to the drone of bees hovering meaninglessly around the late summer roses and the raucous twittering of the resident mockingbird.

"Oh, I wish I could talk with Sunny Monroe. She knew more than she was telling, I'm sure. But I couldn't call her a liar. And then, when the baby miscarried, I had no more ties with her. I never spoke to her again. I knew that she still lived here in town. You know the little stories in the paper about this or that charity or activity or whatnot? I'd see her name or photo and so I know that she was still around. And my mother always read the obits. 'More religiously than a Southern Baptist reads the Bible' was how she put her obsession. If Sunny Monroe had died, at least here in town, we would have noticed it."

Joey picked up her phone that she had placed on the small table. "That is one problem with yoga pants, they don't have pockets for phones. Have you seen my new phone? Does everything, including looking up the phone book. Let's see, Sunny Monroe. Oh, does she have another name? Like Susan? Let's try that." Joey fussed for a few minutes.

"You know, someday we will just say to the phone, 'Call so-and-so' and it will do it. Scary idea. Joey, do you have a phone book?"

"Yeah, in the kitchen by the phone."

Very wandered into the kitchen, found an old one stashed under the phone and looked up Monroe. Under 'S Monroe' was a street address and a number. It looked familiar, so Very took out her phone and dialed.

"Hello," a female voice answered.

"Hi, is this Sunny?" Very asked hesitantly.

"No, this is her daughter, Marty. Who is calling?"

"Very, Vermilion Blew. Do you remember me?"

A pause, then, "Of course I remember. What can I do for you?"

"I know this might seem a bit late to ask, but did you ever hear from Frankie? You know, after he left, did he ever get in touch again?"

"You're right, it is a bit late. But no, we never heard from him. Sweet brother Frankie, vanished for good. So why are you asking now? Too late, isn't it?"

"Did you see the paper this morning? About the body in the orchard?"

"No, I try not to read the silly parts of the paper."

"I've just been to the sheriff's office. I think it may have been Frankie."

"What? Frankie in an orchard? I don't get it."

"Read the paper. I need to talk with your mother, if she's still around and okay with that?"

"Yeah, she's still with us, and I live here with her now. But Frankie, they've found Frankie?"

"No, the body has not been identified, but all the pieces fit. I need some more information and she might have it. Can I come and talk with her?"

"Wait. Not now, call again later, maybe tomorrow. I'll talk to her. She's getting old, you know how it is?"

"I lived with my mother until the end, as well. I know. I'll call tomorrow."

"Listen, let me prepare her a little. This might just kill her off." Marty hung up without saying goodbye.

Chapter Five: A Visit to Sunny Monroe

Very went outside to Joey and said goodbye, "I'm visiting Sunny tomorrow morning. They live in the same place. They, meaning Sunny and Marty, Frankie's younger sister. Thanks for the tea, and the chat. I need to seriously think of moving forward, don't I? I've retired, Mom's gone, what now? But this, this uncertainty..."

"I'm sure everything will turn out; you'll land on your feet, you always do!" Joey gave Very a big hug and a wet kiss on her cheek.

Very walked to her car. If Joey didn't give out so many hugs and kisses to her, which she gave to all of her family and friends as well, Very would only have a cat to give her affection. Everyone needed a Joey in their lives.

When she arrived home, the cat greeted her with a purr and a demand for food. As she poured some kibble for the sturdy, but not fat, cat, Very looked again at the linoleum floor. She remembered when her mother had it installed. Her father had been a bit stingy when it came to renovations on the house, and in the years since he died, her mother had taken on his attitudes. The floor was scuffed. Never a great color, now it looked like puke-green mixed with barf-brown swirls and a feeling of walking on sticky sand. The couch in the family room stood, as it always had, immediately in front of the TV. An afghan hung on the back. She had never liked the colors, or the pattern, but her mother had clung to it because her mother had crocheted it. And Very had left it where her mother had last placed it.

The whole house was crumbling from the inside outwards. That socket didn't work, so don't use it. That lamp stopped working, so what? The refrigerator door water faucet leaked, then quit. And it was never fixed or replaced. 'Do we need a new refrigerator just because the door faucet is broken? Can't you just drink out of the sink?' Every time she tried to call an electrician or a plumber to fix some small thing, her mother objected. Every excuse that she could think of had been offered for not fixing, renovating or getting anything new. Mom had died with a very healthy bank account, and a house in tatters. Very had inherited the house and a sizeable portion of the bank account. Sissy had sneered at her possession of the house, but she knew the neighborhood and the neighbors. It was still valuable real estate. She could renovate now; replace the fridge, the carpet, the couch. Fix the broken sockets. But would that be a good use of money? What about the neighborhood? Was it really the 'desirable' neighborhood that it once was? Would it be worthwhile to spend so much money to renovate here?

Very walked out to the backyard. The sycamore tree that had sprouted tiny green buds in the wedding photo now had giant brown leaves that were rapidly filling the patio. She took a broom and started sweeping.

The next morning's light filtered into Very's closed eyes. 'Now' she told herself and got up. Years of waking early had made sleeping in difficult, even when that was her favorite activity, lying in a warm bed with her eyes closed. She made coffee, in the old coffee maker she had railed against for years. Why couldn't she get a new one? Just drive off to the housewares store and pick out the latest in coffee makers? Why live feeling disgusted with herself every morning?

The newspaper had no more news of the body in the orchard; the sheriff's detective had hinted as much. The obits didn't carry the news of the death of anyone that Very knew, and the rest of the local news was the same infighting of the City Council, the county Board of Supervisors, the Water Board, the Agricultural Boards, the boards of schools, colleges and hospitals. Accusations of corruption, undue influence, gerrymandering, bribery and incompetence spread across the paper on a daily basis. Skip this, she had an errand for the day.

After a quick phone call, Very drove to Frankie Monroe's old house. She hadn't been there but once since the cancelled wedding. She had gone with her mother just four days later, a quick visit to see if there had been any news and to return the simple wedding gift that Sunny Monroe had given them. Marty had been a teenager then and so the conversation was stilted and formal. What do two mature women, a jilted young woman and a teenager talk about? She only remembered the comment about taking after his old man and running, leaving the bad situation. That night, she started having terrible cramps and then lost her baby. No reason to return.

The neighborhood was similar in age to that of Very's parents'. The houses had been built about the same time. The 1952 earthquake had destroyed whole blocks of brick buildings downtown and produced a crop of used bricks that builders and landscapers had scarfed up to reuse on landscaping. Low brick walls lined driveways, and her patio was mostly a mosaic of motley brickwork. An occasional adobe house filled in the rows of diverse styles. The backyards hid expensive landscaped pools, and garages hid classic cars. But as she went south, the streets with no curbs, let alone sidewalks, and the junked cars in the front yards grew in number. The Monroe house was much the same, however. Because this was a county enclave within the city, there were no streetlights. The Monroes had a carriage light in the front yard by the street. Wonder if it worked? Mom's didn't. Very parked her car across the street.

Although Very had spent hours the night before rehearsing what she was going to say, she suddenly had butterflies. Marty had said they were expecting her, but could she ask the right questions? The short conversation the day before had at least prepared them for Frankie being dead, not just missing. Very got out of her car, walked to the front door and knocked.

She heard the sounds of a walker being dragged along a wooden floor. The door squeaked open. "Yes," croaked an ancient's voice.

"Mom, let me help you," came a younger woman's voice.

"Martha, I can do it."

"Oh, am I 'Martha' today?"

The door opened wider, "Hello Very, come in. We are expecting you, despite the confusion," Marty said, holding the screen door open.

Very entered the living room, directly from the porch. To the left was a kitchen and dining room, and directly in front of her was a couch, matching love seat and directly in front of the furniture, was a large screen TV. The house style, the furniture, the layout, all screamed 1955, but the big screen TV was the lone twenty-first century fixture. It seemed to be that way among all of the gently growing older crowd in her hometown.

"Coffee, lemonade, or just water?" Marty asked.

"Oh, lemonade please. It's going to heat up again today, not yet fall weather," Very answered.

Sunny Monroe shuffled her walker to a well dented section of the couch directly in front of the TV; Very sat on the loveseat. "How are you, Mrs. Monroe?"

"That's sweet, Mrs. Monroe. Call me 'Sunny'. How has life treated you, Vermilion Blew?"

"Good. I'm retired now, but I had a great job for years, I was a school librarian here in Bakersfield. I traveled in the summertime, and I lived with my mom. She just died last spring. So, I guess I could say that life has been good."

"Health, that's the most important thing. We hear that when we're young and don't believe it. Old farts, telling us to take care of our health. But, believe me, it's true. How's your health?"

"Great, and I agree with you. I'm now one of the old farts. Health is terribly important."

"Married? Kids? Grandkids by now?"

"No, no and no."

"So, why not?"

Very stared at Sunny Monroe and let the silence speak for her. Long ago, she had learned not to answer these questions. Once again, she handed the rude intrusiveness back to the asker.

Sunny looked at Very with narrowed eyes, taking her measure. "So, what is this about a body in an orchard?"

Before Very could answer, she heard the clink of ice in glasses and waited for Marty to return from the kitchen.

Again, Very started from the beginning: the newspaper story, the ticket found in the pocket, the trip to the Sheriff's Office and the attempt to find some more evidence to identify the body. "I have only one photo, but I thought that you might have more. Do you have dental records, maybe something that could have DNA on it?"

Sunny spoke slowly. "I don't have anything. We moved a lot when the kids were young and when Frankie left home, off to wherever, I threw away anything of his, like where he went to the dentist or the doctor. He had some clothes here, but when we did a clean out about three years after he disappeared, we threw them all out, or gave them to Goodwill."

"You have nothing left from his younger years?" Very persisted.

Both women looked at Very. "No," said Marty. "We just told you."

"I thought, maybe. It's just that, in my house, I have too much stuff from my childhood, my mother's childhood, my sister's childhood, my father's childhood. Way too much stuff. So, I assume that everyone else is in the same boat."

Silence dropped over the living room like a Bakersfield winter fog.

"No, we told you. We have nothing. There may be a few old photos, I have some, but not many, and not terribly useful. I'll try to dig them up if you want. But we have no 'souvenirs', no tangible evidence to help identify the body. I think I know the photo you mean. He had a copy. Just the two of you, close up, smiling, happy?"

Very took the photo out of her purse and showed them. They looked closely, faces closed, no emotion. "And you had no idea where he might have gone? You never heard anything from him, or about him? Friends say anything?"

"Nope," said Marty. "Nothing, ever."

"Just like his dad," cut in Sunny. "I knew he had done the same thing his father did. Walked out. Never came back."

Marty took over the story. "I'll tell you like I was told. Shortly after I was born, I'm four years younger than Frankie, Dad left. He avoided the responsibility of a kid, another kid to be raised."

"He owed someone money," Sunny cut in. "The guy came to collect late one night. I'd never seen him before, and Mr. Monroe wasn't at home. I managed to get him to leave. Little one here," she nodded towards Marty, "was screaming a blue streak. Little kids screaming like that always scare big bullies. He left and never came back, but there were some slashed tires and a rock through a window. Anyway, Big Mr. Monroe skipped out. I heard him one night, outside, arguing with someone. That was the night he left. I tried to ask him where he was going, but he told me it was better that I didn't know."

"So, he just disappeared? Never saw him again?" Very sat, fascinated by the tale.

"Oh, I heard from him. It was all about money. Monroe gave me $500 in cash as he was heading out the door. He told me to hide it, $10 here, $20 there, and to go easy on it. He said to not spend it all at the same time. I guess he figured that the guy he owed money to would be looking to take it off me if he knew I had it. If I just spent a bit here and a bit there, he wouldn't suspect that I actually had some cash worth taking. So, I did that. We were living in Redding at the time. Thank God I had my parents and a brother who could help me out. And give me a reason to say that I had enough for groceries and the rent. But after a while, even that began to run out. Then I got a cashier's check in the mail. Enough to tide me over for a while. Never a phone call or a letter. And then, out of the blue, another check. After a year or year and a half, even that stopped. He never contacted me, or his lovely baby daughter again.

"We moved, a lot. I was a hair dresser. Best job ever for making a little cash here and there. I'd do home perms for $5, simple kid's cuts for $2. If we were settled for a while, I'd get a chair in a salon. More stable."

"One of my first memories is sweeping hair for a quarter," laughed Marty.

"We always had a place to live, food on the table. Everyone was healthy. I had nothing to complain of. As I said, my parents were always happy to help a little. Christmas was always good because of them. But the two kids were a handful, especially Marty here. High school was hard on her. Frankie had always been her protector, but when he graduated from high school, he went a-wandering. And Marty lost the protection and guidance of her big brother. Drink, marijuana, boys. What do you do with a teenager like that?"

"Hey, I made it, didn't I?" Marty countered. "I'm here, taking care of you. Where would you be without me? In one of those smelly old folks' homes, with a bunch of Nurse Ratchetts and nasty old men chasing you around the hallways?" She smiled at Very. "She spent three months in a place like that. I brought her home, here, and I've taken care of her ever since. Not exciting, living with your divorced daughter, but better than a 'home'."

"Yes, I guess you've been a good daughter. But oh, that Frankie! He could be a handful too, but he was a charmer. He'd bring home a note from school and then he'd smile and talk his way out of it. Everyone else was wrong about the other kid with the black eye, the cheating on a quiz or some such thing. He could have broken your heart, but you would have loved him for it. You know that, Very. He did it to you too."

Chapter Six: What Sunny Knew

Very was stunned. She had not known that to be accepted by one's future mother-in-law was a crucial thing. The mother-in-law jokes were there for a reason: to help everyone negotiate the clinging, controlling, conniving, domineering, interfering, argumentative, disapproving mother of one's spouse. Now, Very understood that Sunny Monroe was offering empathy and understanding of what might have been. She had understood her little boy; how manipulative, but charming, he could be. And now she sympathized with Very's situation. After all, she had experienced life with Frankie's father, who had pulled a similar episode on her. She knew what it was like to be left high and dry, with a baby to take care of. This empathy, this sympathy and bond had never been what she expected from Sunny Monroe.

"Yes, he broke my heart, but I guess I've forgiven him. The years that have passed have made it seem too much like another life. This life, now, is what I am, and how I define myself. Love him, though? I can't answer that. It's like I've put it all into a bottle and thrown it into the sea. The thoughts, the feelings, everything that was, is gone," Very said simply and quietly.

"Why are you here? What can I do?" Sunny shifted uncomfortably in her perch on the couch.

"I have this picture," Very said placing the picture on the coffee table between them. "But nothing else. I was hoping that you had something, anything that could identify him. Maybe I just want to put the nails in the coffin, make sure it's him and then we can all get on with life."

"We have got on with life, it's you who needs to pound some nails. But I told you, we threw out everything when he left. We've got nothing of his anymore." Sunny snorted softly.

"Not even a birth certificate? A school report card? I can understand about dental records, we really don't keep anything like that, but surely, there is something that might help us identify him?" Very felt angry and frustrated. She might have had reason to erase Frankie from her life, but what about these two? What had he done to them to deserve to be so forgotten and ignored? "DNA? That's what you have."

A stillness welled up from the very depths of the dusty carpets and swirled around the room.

"Ah, I didn't think of that," Sunny said finally.

"It wouldn't do any good," Marty added.

"You mean you would refuse to give DNA if that was the only way to identify your son, your brother? Why? It doesn't even hurt to give DNA." Very said with mounting frustration. "How could you refuse such a simple request? How could you stand in the way of knowing this was Frankie?"

"Oh, no, I'm not afraid of giving DNA. And I'm not refusing," Marty said. "It's just that it wouldn't do any good."

"I know it is expensive and I am sure we can get around that. After all, the police need to identify the body and they can pay for it. We can explain about the dental records and all," Very countered.

"No, you don't understand. It's just that it wouldn't prove anything. I'm not Frankie's sister." Marty looked at Very with a wide-eyed look and a sly smile on her face. "We're not related."

Very looked at Sunny for confirmation of this. Sunny looked enigmatic.

"And you? We can get your DNA, right?" Very waited for the answer and felt unquiet as the reticence lingered.

"I may have raised the boy, but I'm not his mother, his real mother, that is." Sunny looked at Very with wide eyes. "He came along with Monroe. And who is gonna turn away a child that needs someone?"

Very looked from one to the other. "I need to get this straight. Monroe is your father, Marty?"

"As far as I know. Mom, is he my dad?" Marty looked saucily at her mother, waiting for her confirmation.

"Yes, Marty, he is your dad. But he told me that he wasn't Frankie's dad. I kept that to myself, hid it from Marty for years," Sunny turned to Very to make sure she was following.

Marty took up the story. "It was when I moved back in a few years ago. I got divorced, my kids had left home and didn't want to know me. Mom here was in a bad way, needing some help. Easy decision, it was. Easy to make, difficult to undo. But when I moved in, there was a lot of junk. That's when I chucked out the rest of it. There may have been some of Frankie's stuff left, but it was mixed in with a bunch of my old clothes and stuff, her old junk, some of my boys' stuff, a cousin's who had briefly stayed here. Just a bunch of crap. I needed to do that. Just so I could have a place to breathe. There weren't any 'documents' if that's what you are looking for. Mom would have those, wouldn't you?"

"If Frankie 'came with Monroe', wasn't he the father?" Very asked.

"I think I wanted to believe he was. I fell for that man, hook, line and sinker. He was a charmer, that's how come I can understand about Frankie. But one day, near the end, when we had a fight, he told me that the kid was a bastard, and not his. But they were so alike in some ways, and I just ignored that. Then when Monroe left, I was stuck with Frankie. I thought Monroe felt that his former lady had cheated on him. He couldn't reject Frankie, but he couldn't own him either."

"What about a birth certificate? Didn't Frankie have a birth certificate? At least it would have his mother's name and a father's name, usually." Very had seldom met such a convoluted life story and was trying to get her head around the details, which seemed to squirm and dodge away from her understanding.

"Well, nowadays I guess it would be nigh on impossible to get by without a piece of paper. School, driver's license, social security card, but back then, people had a tendency to take your word for it. Or you could use one identity to prove another. When I took him to school, it was easy. I just told them his birth date, which seemed fine since he looked like a five-year-old. I did a good job of choosing a date. You know, some kids get stuck with a holiday date and then their birthday always gets lost in the celebration. I knew a kid when I was young, born on Christmas Eve. What a terrible day. Never had a proper birthday, always stuck in with Christmas. 'Oh, you don't need two presents, I just got you one for both days!' That's what she heard all her life. So, I always gave her three presents, just to make up for all the other presents she missed. I even had the nerve to tell her mother to her face that she was a bad mother for having her daughter at Christmas. I was so mad for my friend. She was good about it, though. She said she would try really, really hard not to have any children on a holiday. Frankie got a good day, March 12, don't you think? And his birth place, I made that one up. I chose a small town in Idaho. I could always tell them the courthouse had a fire. They didn't question me. Frankie told them that once, and because it was a sad story, they just believed it.

"And then, I used that school record for everything else, for the next school and the next doctor and so on. You come at somebody with a whole passel of papers that all say the same thing, well, you got it made. So, Frankie got a birthday, a mother, me, a daddy, Old Man Monroe and a place to come from. He never remembered anything before me, so he was okay with it. He never questioned anything."

"But what about that blood test? That one in high school, where we were looking at all of our family and learning about genetics and blood types?" Marty interrupted. "You knew all along, didn't you? Daaaamn." She laughed at her mother's deception.

"Silly things about school. You don't need to know anybody's blood type but your own," Sunny said.

"But you and I have the same, O positive, I think. Really common. But Frankie's was different, something so weird that only 1% of the people have it. Someone said that Mom couldn't have been Frankie's mother if they had such different blood types. But that was after Frankie graduated from high school and left. He was back for a weekend, so I took some blood from him, for the class project. But he was gone by the time we had done all the tests, so I never got to tell him. But then again, someone suggested that he had substituted someone else's blood. But I know it was his, I took it. He was a big baby about it. 'Owww, owww'. I had wondered about that for years, but after a while, more important things in life came up, so. But after Mom told me that Frankie wasn't hers, or Old Man Monroe's, well, there it is. It hasn't changed anything, really. He left and never came back. But in thinking about the blood test, I believe it was true. He has nothing genetically to do with either of us. And so, DNA can't help you."

"And if you have nothing with his DNA on it, clothes or anything, then that is that."

The three women sat companionably silent for a minute, each lost in thoughts of the vanished Frankie.

"He was my son, though. I raised him, I helped him through all the scrapes with his teachers, the bullying from the bigger kids. I enjoyed his charm, his way of telling stories about everyone, even about himself. There was the time the cops caught him with fire crackers in that vacant lot. They picked him up. He should have gone to juvie, but they let me take him home. God, he smiled at them and apologized in that funny hoarse voice of his, that always sounded older than his years, like a grown-up, even when he was a kid. Nobody could resist his charm. And that little bit of hair that would fall onto his forehead and curl. Whooo boy." Sunny sighed.

But Very laughed. "Here's one for you. 'There was a little girl, who had a little curl, right in the middle of her forehead. When she was good, she was very, very good, and when she was bad she was horrid.' My dad used to say that to me. I didn't exactly have a curl in the middle of my forehead, like Frankie did. And I was a good girl, for the most part."

"Unlike our Frankie," Marty added.

"Did Frankie know that you weren't his mother?" Very asked.

"I never told him to his face, but maybe he thought something was wrong. I mean, he didn't look unlike either of us, just not really like us. His hair was darker, but so what? His skin was the same color. And besides, how can you tell? I never treated him differently. He had a family, just not related to him. He never starved, or went without. And what is love of a family if not that?" Sunny looked at Very for confirmation.

"What about that fight you two had a couple of nights before the wedding? Money, wasn't it?" Marty reminded Sunny.

"That was nothing. He wanted some money. Said he was getting married and they needed things and he had some bills to pay. I gave him a $100, but he wanted more. I didn't have it, frankly, and I didn't want to give it to him, directly. I wanted to give it to the two of you. You both needed it, so if you were getting married, you should get it together. But he wanted it." Sunny fell silent.

"Do you think that's why he left? He owed someone money?" Very leaned over to talk directly to Sunny. "Did he say who he owed money to, and what for? He never said anything to me about owing money. I had a little and my parents were going to give us a lot, to help, you know, with the baby and stuff." Very went silent as she realized that this was the first time she had mentioned the baby, although both knew about it, and the loss less than a week later. "No, money couldn't have been a problem. All he needed was to ask me."

"Did he leave because he found out Mom wasn't his Mom, and I wasn't his sister? Could he have been really mad and disappointed and wanted to get out? I never rejected him, but I wasn't close to him, especially when we got older." Marty sighed at the thought. "I didn't treat him like anything but a brother, ever. It wouldn't have mattered to me if he wasn't biologically related to me. I would have, I did, accept him as a member of my family."

"How could he have found out if I didn't tell him? Old Man Monroe show up and spill the beans? That's an idea out of the blue." Sunny sighed tiredly.

"But he wasn't without a family. He knew the baby was his. Even if he had found out the woman who raised him wasn't his mother, and his sister wasn't his sister, he was making his own family. His own biological child was on the way. He was excited about becoming a father. No, he didn't leave for that reason. What reason could he have left for? No," Very said forcefully, slamming her hand down on the chair arm. "It was not about finding out his parents weren't his parents. That's not a good reason to leave. No, he didn't leave. He was murdered!"

Chapter Seven: Who Is Frankie Monroe?

Very stood in preparation to take her leave. "I'm in touch with the sheriff's department. They may contact you, but I'll tell them what you said about the DNA. And I'll tell them about dental records, and how things stand with you guys, no records, no possessions etc. You don't have to do that. Is there anything else you can tell me that would help in identifying the body? Old injuries, like broken bones and things?"

Sunny sat on the end of the couch, clearly tired out from the encounter with the past. Very sympathized. She had seen her mother flag when people came to visit, demanding that she play 'recall the past' with them. Very resented the way people put their own agendas before those of the clearly aging; people who had a short attention span, challenges with memory, physical disabilities.

Marty shrugged. "I can't think of anything, maybe Mom can. But later, another time, huh? She's just 'plum wore out' as my grandma used to say. And I can tell it's time to take your pills, isn't it, you old lady."

"Yes, I can see that. I'll keep in touch. Maybe I should have kept in touch?" Very said. "Maybe it would have been polite, and…"

"No," Marty said. "You didn't need to. No reason to. If Frankie had shown up, out of the blue, or called, or something, I think we knew where you were, or how to get in touch. I guess we were all just waiting for something to happen, for some movement. And then…the years slipped by."

"Well, this may be it. Bye for now." Very held the screen door gently so it wouldn't bang behind her and walked to her car. She felt eyes boring into her back, but she refused to turn around.

Back home, Very called the Sheriff's office and left a long message for Detective Williams, who couldn't answer the phone. She didn't really care if she talked to him or not. She had nothing to add and the only thing to say was that Sunny and Marty Monroe were dead ends. She also asked Detective Williams to not call them directly, if possible, as Mrs. Monroe was ailing.

Very made herself some tea and carried it out to the back yard. As soon as she sat down, the detective called her back. She repeated her story and apologized to the detective. "I know we need more concrete proof than the theater ticket. I tried to make it easier, but this is a setback."

"Don't worry, we are still working on it. We have other avenues. This isn't your problem to solve. It's ours."

Very put the phone down. Sorrow fell over her. She retrieved the 'wedding photos' and looked at them again. She had carried his child, albeit for a short time. They had been linked biologically, the only person she knew who was linked to Frankie that way. What about Sunny and Marty? They were the mother and sister of a man who was gone and whom they couldn't even claim any kinship to. Of course, they had lived with him for years; he called them Mom and Sis. And did he ever know, or suspect? Marty had started to tell a story of blood types, but had never really finished it. Frankie had had an extremely unusual blood type, but even unusual blood types were inherited. That didn't prove anything. But did he know about this? Marty had been unclear whether Frankie had stuck around after he had forked over the blood. Of course, Sunny knew the relationship. But had Frankie ever found out? She hadn't asked. She should have pressed Sunny on this question, but the time hadn't been right.

Sad or angry? What did it mean to know that her fiancé, father of her child, had been murdered? She had never known a murdered person, not personally. They showed up daily in the papers, it seemed at the rate of one day in Bakersfield. But she had never met any of them – before now. What did it mean to the family of the murdered? Someone gone, yes, but more than that. People died all the time. Even horrible things like accidents are common enough, let alone strokes and heart attacks. One day the person is here, the next day, he's gone. But murder. Deliberate, violent, often face-to-face. And most often someone you know. Frankie, the father of her poor lost baby, a murder victim. A tear slipped out of her eye and trickled down her cheek, leaving a salty trail of loss and remorse. For the baby. For Frankie. For herself.

Had she loved him? Was that the same as being charmed by him? What had Sunny said about charming everyone? She closed her eyes and tried to conjure up a vision of a living, breathing Frankie, one who put his arms around her and kissed her with such softness and tenderness. Had he done that because he was being charming, or did he love her? What is love anyway? If someone likes you and treats you well, aren't you likely to love them? When does love start? Can there be love at first sight? She didn't believe that you could fall in love with someone without knowing them, well. But she hadn't known Frankie well. Did she know him at all? She had always been so level headed and sure of herself. Had she failed that time? Had his charm sent her off her rails? Why was it that when she got pregnant she decided to marry so quickly? She was sure of herself, she knew that. She knew that this was going to be a good match. He wasn't as educated as she, but he was sharp and intelligent. He had read some of the classics and he read current events in the newspaper. He could use the English language accurately and often with a flair that she lacked. Colorful phrases and inventive jokes poured from him. Everyone liked his colorful turn of phrase, and laughed with him. He was charming. But she had also been sure at the time that he was real, and honest.

But did she know much about him? Sunny and Marty had hinted that he had left home as soon as he had graduated from high school in Redding. Or was that when he finished school? Finished with school? He had talked about college classes, so she was sure he had stopped somewhere long enough to enroll. But he had talked about playing a musical instrument and helping out with a band as well. Jobs here and there, trying out professions, he had called it. Was this meandering, this restlessness, a search for his father and mother? She heard Sunny's words again, "Old Man Monroe left when Marty was a baby." What were the nuances in that sentence? What had Frankie said to her about his father? Dredging up memories wasn't any easier each time she did it. She listened in her head for his voice. The deep, rolling throaty voice saying, "Old Man Monroe left when Marty was a baby."

The fog returned. Had she misremembered? Who had said this? How had they said this? As she felt fainter and fainter, she put her head down on her knees, leaning far forward, trying to stop the feeling of nausea and impending loss of consciousness. "Yeah, Old Man Monroe left when Marty was a baby," he said, the sound coming from the fog. She was sure that it was he who had said it, exactly like that. And now, he said it again out of the fog that filled her head. She bent forward more and breathed deeply and evenly. Gradually, the feeling dissipated, and the voice receded.

When she felt more herself, she called Joey. "News update," Very announced. She told Joey what had transpired at the Monroe house and the bombshell Sunny Monroe had dropped on her. "So, no records at all, especially dental records, which are valuable. And no DNA because neither is related to Frankie. Where does that leave me?"

They discussed the ramifications of this and then Joey opined, "Maybe we'll never know who the body is, for sure, that is."

"And then, I heard his voice. Of course, I haven't heard him speak in 37 years, but it sounded as though he was right there," Very said. "I was trying to remember what he had said about his Dad, something that Sunny said today. And then, I could hear him, clearly, like he was sitting right beside me. 'Old Man Monroe left when Marty was a baby.' A ghost? But I don't believe in ghosts."

"No, it wasn't a ghost. It was your clever and creative imagination. Forget it."

"I am neither clever nor imaginative. But in this case, a good memory, a very good one," Very said.

"You do have an extraordinary memory, but you are also clever and imaginative. I think we need a new conversation about the assets of one Vermilion Blew. Don't discount your strengths. But forget the ghostly conversations with a long dead man."

"So, you do believe the body is Frankie?" Very asked.

"I don't have all the facts, but it seems pretty likely to me," Joey said.

"Has your hubby said anything?"

"Very, you know he can't, he works for the Sheriff's Department for heavens' sake. And I believe that in this case, he is trying to stay very far away, given the connection between us. Do not ask again, okay?" Joey's gritted teeth could be heard over the phone lines.

"Sorry, sorry. I just thought if it was public, he could say something."

"You are right, if it were public. But nothing yet, I promise. Talk to you tomorrow, okay?"

"Yeah, bye." Very hung up and then checked the time. Too early for a call to her sister. Instead, she cleaned house.

Soft sunlight kissed the back yard and Very took her cup of tea, sufficiently cooled, to sip on the lounge chair. The housecleaner had been let go when her mother died, and Very had done minimal cleaning since then. There had been time this summer to get to the nooks and crannies and clean them out. Unfortunately, she had only gotten as far as the kitchen.

She checked her phone. Five-thirty, Sissy would be home from work. Now that her kids had left home, she knew that Sissy was sitting on the couch with a glass of wine, unwinding from her workday.

"Hey Sissy," Very said as soon as her sister had answered. "What kind of wine are you drinking tonight?"

"How'd you know that I had a glass of wine?"

"You're my little sister. It is my job to know what you are up to. And I have found you oh-so-many times having a glass at this time of day. So, what kind?" Very laughed.

"Cheap chardonnay. But why have you called?"

"You said that you would come and help clean out the junk and take what you want. It's been about four months now, if you can believe it, and I am getting antsy to get started. So, when can you come?"

"It's about time you got around to cleaning out stuff. It's just flat-out creepy you living in that house alone with all of her stuff. What prompted you now, today? Spring cleaning in the fall?"

"No, a body in an orchard. Just outside Bakersfield."

"Nothing unusual about that, though. Very, you are not making sense."

Very sighed, "They think it might be Frankie Monroe."

Silence swelled into the absence of sound, of talk, of platitudes.

"The Frankie Monroe that jilted you when you were pregnant? Why do they think that?"

"There was a ticket in the pocket. The part that was left made them realize it was from the Nile Theatre, the Friday night before the wedding. We went to the movies," Very said.

"And no one has heard from him since?" Sissy added.

"I visited his mother and sister. They still live here, in the same house."

"Damned weird. And how did he die? Accident, suicide or…?"

"Murder? I don't think they know yet, but it looks suspiciously like murder. You don't bury yourself, and the body has been there for a while."

"So, what are you going to do?"

"I'm cleaning up the house. The body has made me think of cleaning up my life, starting with our mother's leftovers."

"My sister, the metaphorical librarian. Only you could link these things! So, what do I want? What can I have?" Sissy turned practical.

"Sissy, I don't have kids, I have no need for 'heirlooms,' so anything in the way of family-oriented stuff should go to you. Your kids need to inherit it."

Sissy guffawed. "My kids? Heirlooms? 'Family oriented' things? That'll be the day that I faint dead away. You know kids nowadays. They care nothing for family. It's all about money, electronics, cars, clothes, out to dinner, drinks, concerts, vacations. It's all frivolity and hedonism. They don't give a shit about the past."

"That is really too bad. Right now, my past is all I have. And it is cursing me."

Chapter Eight: Identification

Very could not manage to pin Sissy down to a date to come and claim her inheritance. But mentally, she immediately started thinking of what Sissy should take for her children. Obviously, since she was out of state, it was too much to expect her to want furniture, but there were glass ornaments, pottery collections, papers, books, and all sorts of miscellaneous 'treasures' that Very was prepared to foist on her sister. If Sissy didn't want them, good; they could be thrown on the trash heap. Too bad her culture did not have a tradition of burning a deceased person's belongings with them.

Very grabbed a cardboard box from the patio, turned it upside down and wiped out the dirt and a few cobwebs. Three wriggling earwigs fell out. "Euww," she squeaked. She wasn't fond of earwigs, but her mother had hated them. 'Worse than cockroaches', she had called them. Giving the box an extra 'thump', she carried it into the guest room. She tried to pull open a drawer to an old dresser. It had been painted a weird shade of blue, bright and cheerful, but weird. Very had gone off to college and Sissy had claimed the room they had shared. She wanted to change the décor and this was the shade she had chosen. The paint had chipped on the edges, revealing a white and an orange shade from its former lives. The drawers had always stuck, but now she wiggled and jiggled it to get the drawer open. She vowed not to close it with anything in it so that she would never have to open it again.

Inside was a jumble of old clothes, paint-spattered, mud-stained and ripped at the elbows and knees. She said, "Holy crapola," and dropped the box, retrieving a plastic bag from the pantry instead. "Garbage city," she muttered, filling the bag. The rest of the dresser was the same. Clothes and rags from another life erupted from the drawers as she captured them in a series of plastic bags. Stopping only for a cup of soup and some crackers, she went on into the night, ripping and tearing at the shreds of her former life. At one point, she spotted an ancient suitcase. The latches were even rustier than the one that contained her wedding mementoes. Once she had it open, she realized that it contained some clothes from her high school days. Who had kept these? Bell-bottom jeans, way too small. Mini-skirts that made her blush at the thought that she had actually worn them. Faded tee-shirts with logos, patterns and colors from the era of day-glo and cutsie.

At midnight, Very stepped back and surveyed her piles of plastic bags. Nothing to keep? She vowed to leave them until the morning to chuck in the garbage cans in the alleyway. She took a quick shower to wash off the dirt, the sweat, and the memories of the past.

Her first sleep was easy. Her muscles were tired and when she relaxed, sleep gripped her immediately. But then, she woke. There were noises in the night; trains whoo-whooed like owls in the distance, garbage cans rumbled in the alleyway, the neighborhood dogs yapped and woofed and, most annoying of all, teenagers gunned their engines and created piercing screeches as they laid black doughnuts in the intersections. Did they need the thrill of the extra-loud engine sounds to accompany their raging testosterone? The trains were doing their job, the garbage cans were being raided by the homeless and poor looking for recyclables that they could redeem, and the dogs were just obeying their natures. But the teenagers had a choice, and that angered her.

She got up and wandered the house. They had moved here when she was a teenager. The La Cresta neighborhood had a cachet even in those days. It was up on the hill, above the fog and bad air. The streets were laid out in meandering lanes, gradually rising to the top at Panorama Drive. There, one could stand on the edge of the bluffs and look out over the oil fields. At night, the lights twinkled on the refineries and bobbing pumpjacks, and if the wind were away from the city, one could avoid the stench. During the day, the walking path along the bluff edge attracted all kinds of citizens, from the dedicated walkers and kids on roller blades to the homeless and those who wished to dump their trash in a neighborhood not their own.

The street outside the house suddenly lit up with the headlights of a passing car. Very peeked out through the blinds and saw a sedan, dark and mysterious, drive by slowly. It could be security, or thieves. She turned on a small reading lamp and picked up an old magazine. She lounged on the couch, flipping the pages, not taking in the contents. Instead, her mind dwelt on the house. Her mother's house. It wasn't a particularly special house, but her mother had thought differently. It was 'her' house. Over the years, and especially in the last ten, as her mother had been more and more unable to keep up the house, she had taken over running the place. At first, her mother didn't want anyone from outside to come and clean, but Very had hired a woman to come once a month and give everything a good cleaning. At first, her mother refused to allow the vacuum cleaner into her room, saying she would do it herself. But after six months, when no vacuum had touched the carpet, the old woman had relented. She had quietly seethed at the control her mother exerted. Every time she mentioned that she would like to think of finding her own place, her mother had whined and bullied her. "What kind of a daughter are you to leave your mother alone after all these years? Why would you want your own place, the hassle of rent, of finding furniture? This place is so nice, with a pool and everything. You have a great deal, why would you want the expense? Besides, you would be over here every day cooking for me, why would you want to cook just for yourself?" They were arguments that made sense, mixed in with the expectation that she needed to take care of her mother as she declined in health and capacity to care for herself. Mother had succeeded. She had stayed. And now, she was alone, facing old age by herself, in the house that her mother had created. Very found an afghan and pulled it up over her legs as she stretched out on the couch.

Another car drove slowly up the street, but this one was accompanied by the faint, but growing louder, 'pop' as newspapers landed in front yards and driveways. When she heard the unmistakable plop on the driveway, she sighed. Did she want to jump up and retrieve it and read the day's news before dawn, or curl up?

Very woke on the couch with the morning sunshine in her face. Her cat jumped up and started to groom her hair, a sign that it was high time to start the day. Very started her morning routine; she made coffee, fed the cat, washed her face, and brought in the newspaper. She approached her closet and scanned the contents. Junk clothes and good clothes. There were no in-betweens. Since she retired, really long before, she had resisted buying new clothes with the idea that she had no place to wear them. If she needed something nice, she had plenty of perfectly good, clean, well-fitting outfits to wear. And if she were lounging around the house, she had shorts and sweats and paint-spattered comfortable old things. Today, the day she was going to haul junk and clean out closets, was an old clothes day. She flipped the hangers in her closet. She found a pair of clean, but worn, khakis. They were at least 25 years old. She slipped them on. They fit. Think of that, the figure of a 35-year-old.

She went to the kitchen and made coffee. She picked up the paper and turned to the obituary page. Halfway through the list of recently deceased, she stopped. She put the paper down and sighed heavily. "No obituaries, I am not my mother." She turned to the front page and groaned. Government shenanigans, impossible choices regarding foreign policy, Democrats and Republicans fighting, and boring stories about pseudo-celebrities. The local page had more of the same. The City Council was still up in arms about the freeway extension, the rise in crime and homelessness and the County Board of Supervisors had tied themselves into pretzels over the renewed attempts to attract new businesses to Bakersfield and Kern County. She talked to the paper, smacking it in the ersatz fight against the ruling elites of the place. "How can you attract business with illiterate and unskilled workers? Education, education! And lordie, I tried." She put the paper down.

She made toast, and cut up a peach that was the last of the season, then poured a cup of coffee. She picked up the paper again, found the funnies and didn't laugh. Was it her, or the day's offerings? She never knew if she laughed because they were truly funny, or if it was her day to day mood. She fetched jam and almond butter from the fridge, found a flowered plate and took her breakfast to the table. She had started using her mother's 'wedding set' since the old woman had died. Her mother had whined that it was too good to use for everyday, but twice a year use had meant the set was still at sixteen strong: dinner, salad, and dessert plates; soup and dessert bowls; coffee and tea cups with matching saucers, as well as three platters, four vegetable serving bowls, soup tureen, gravy boat, milk and sugar servers and a series of little liver shaped dishes that her mother had insisted were 'places to put bones'. She had countered that they were sauce dishes. But the set took up three shelves, piled high. Now, she had liberated a few plates to use for her breakfast. She felt deliciously wicked and gloated every time she touched them. "Beautiful little plates," she told her cat.

She went back to the paper. The local section was always good for some gossip about people she knew. New store openings and old closings, crimes and misdemeanors, kudos and awards. "Body identified." The article sat at the bottom in the far-right hand corner, only two columns wide. Very stared at the headlines for a full minute. This was it. They were going to tell her that Frankie Monroe was dead. This was the notification that she had been dreading, but expecting, for days. Perhaps for years. She had told herself that she had forgotten about Frankie, but this was proof that she had not. Deep inside her head, there was always the little voice that told her she had been left at the altar because she wasn't good enough. That she lost her baby because she was incapable of being a mother. She had lived with these ideas all her life, while not admitting it and denying it if asked. Over the years, the idea had gone dormant, for weeks or months at a time, but had never disappeared. Now, a new time had come. Frankie had not left her, he had been murdered. How was she going to incorporate this idea, write a new narrative, and live beyond the dark thoughts that had gone on for so long?

Cautiously, she read the article. She skimmed the words, hardly taking them in. She looked for a name, some indication of confirmation. She read 'dental records' and 'missing person's report'. She stopped reading and shook her head. What? What was happening? There were no dental records, unless someone else had supplied them. She had talked with his mother, who said she had no idea who the dentist was. And a report? What report? Who filed it? Sunny and Marty had both said that no report had been filed. They had just thought he had walked out like Old Man Monroe. They had not made a report. So who did? Was there another family? Maybe he had walked out on her because he was already married? Maybe the other wife had reported him missing? But when? How did she know?

Very turned back to the article, reading carefully instead of skimming. She read it carefully, word by word. 'Body' and 'orchard', the day it was found, five days ago now. 'Identified' and 'positively' using 'dental records'. Based on a 'missing person's report' filed in 1973 by the wife of the deceased. Sheriff's Department treating it as a 'homicide.' Her mouth filled with a metallic taste and her stomach churned. Then she read, "The deceased was positively identified as Daniel Harger, late of Bakersfield."

It wasn't Frankie. The dead man with the ticket in his pocket was not her Frankie. But who was Daniel Harger?

Chapter Nine: Who Was Frankie Monroe – Really?

Very's coffee cup slipped and crashed to the floor. Not Frankie Monroe. Then, where is he? Not dead, at least not this body.

Very shook her head in the realization that she had been counting on this corpse being that of Frankie. That would have solved a lot of questions. It would have meant that she could put all kinds of things behind her for good. She could have closed this chapter of her life and moved on, really moved on. But now, it was not to be.

She dialed Sissy's number. It rang and rang. Finally, the answering machine message came on and Very left a short and cryptic announcement, "I'm cleaning out." Very thought that would light a fire under her sister. She hoped that the tension in her voice and the finality of the words would serve as a red flag. Sissy needed to get her act in order. Sissy needed to realize that Mom was gone and that the detritus of her life would soon begin to disperse. In the end, it was up to Very to take the initiative, but she had now done it, issued the challenge. They both knew that when she started the cleaning process, she would call the shots. Sissy needed to hurry up and make her wishes known. What did she want out of their mother's worldly goods?

Very skittered around the kitchen, cleaning the counter tops. Then she started scooping up her mother's things. The first to come to hand was a garden gnome that was too small for the garden. It was only four inches high. Where would anyone put a gnome this size? Where did it come from? And why had it been sitting on the counter for all these months? Or was it years?

Very replaced the gnome on the counter and looked around for a box. She wandered around the house and finally grabbed the key to the garage. The garage door lock stuck and she had to tug and twist to open it. At least having a sticky lock might deter a burglar, if they couldn't pick the lock to get inside. She stepped into the garage and took a look around. No room for a car in this two-car garage. Piles of old pool supplies lay in boxes, in loose piles and hung on the walls. A pair of overalls that had belonged to her dad hung on the wall. She backed out. Her dad had been gone for well over 30 years. Why was this item still here? Why couldn't it have been thrown away, given away, packed away? She cursed the Daughter of the Depression and made a note to buy boxes.

Back in the kitchen she poured herself another cup of coffee. Then she slumped forward, head on the table. What was she doing this for? What was her motivation for cleaning up now? What was on her mind that was forcing her to clean, sweep, get rid of the past? Obviously, there was the non-starter of the body being Frankie, but nothing had changed. He was still missing; his body was not found. Shouldn't that be the end of something, not the beginning of a great clean-out?

She called Joey. She always called Joey when things went awry. Joey know how to tell her she was full of shit or full of made-up anxieties. She muttered to herself. "I'm not usually the one to call Joey. It's Joey who usually calls me, with the same varied set of problems, anxieties and fears of not making the right choices." The phone rang on and on. She got the answering machine. "Hi, Joey. It's me." She hung up. Where was everyone today, not attached to their phones? Now that everyone had mobile phones, why didn't they hang around with them in their pockets, to answer immediately?

She warmed up the coffee in the microwave. She was prepared for the body to be that of Frankie. She welcomed the idea of his being dead. Then she could put it all to rest. Even though he would be dead, murdered even, at least she could say that was the reason for his non-appearance at the wedding. It wouldn't be that he had walked out on her; it was that he couldn't make it. Her idea of Frankie had turned around in the last couple of days. She had always thought that he was a rat who abandoned her and the baby. Or alternately, that he was not man enough to take on the responsibility, or scared about the burdens of being a husband and father. When Sunny had told her that he had left like his own (non) father did, she had accepted that. He had run away. That notion did not make her happy, but it was an explanation. Now, what was the explanation?

Was he still out there? He was only a year or so older than she, so he was quite likely to still be alive. But where? And why was there never any trace of him? Being left at the altar was not that uncommon, but most men didn't disappear entirely. They just got cold feet. So, if he wasn't the man in the orchard, but the man in the orchard had a ticket for that night's movie in his pocket, what was the connection? Maybe Frankie was killed too. Maybe his body was still out there, just a few feet away. Both of them killed, because they were both at the movie, but one of them found, the other still buried in that orchard.

Very jumped up and looked for the newspapers, both of them. Where was that orchard? She flipped through the papers. The first article did not mention where the orchard was. The second time, the paper mentioned Delano. Delano, where in Delano? The place was surrounded by orchards. When she was young, it was all cotton and alfalfa. Now, it was table grapes and orchards. Millions of trees, as far as the eye could see. People came from LA to have their engagement and wedding photos taken under the white and pale pink canopy of almond trees in bloom. It could resemble snow on March first, an unlikely scenario in this part of California, but a lovely background for photos. The exact location was missing from the articles.

How many orchards were there near Delano? Maybe if she went there and drove around, she could spot the one whose trees were being ripped out for replanting? There couldn't be that many at this moment, could there?

"If I say this out loud, it sounds really, really stupid," said Very out loud. "How many orchards near Delano?"

She couldn't ask the sheriff. It wasn't her man, so they wouldn't tell her anything except what was in the paper. So how could she find out what happened?

She sat at the table and pulled a pad of paper towards her. She rummaged for a working pen, and then started the list. List-making was a Very specialty. It was in her DNA, she was convinced. The list for Santa was the first list she ever made, with the help of her dad. As soon as she could write herself, she was listing, categorizing, sorting, classifying, grouping, and organizing everything. If you wanted information, she could find it in her dictionary, thesaurus, encyclopedia and then in the reference books in the library. There was never a doubt as to her career. She was an organized finder of information. A librarian.

She started the list with the question, "Who was Frankie Monroe?" Perhaps that wasn't even the name on his birth certificate. But she had no other name, not even a middle name, for the man who won and lost her heart. The next question, "Why did he disappear?"

This question was at least as difficult as the first. The obvious one, he didn't want to get married and was afraid to tell her, was written immediately under the question. Start with the obvious, she thought. But Very immediately drew a line, not too heavy, through this answer. She had thought long about this in the days after the fiasco. She had thought of little else, until the cramps and then the hospital visit intruded and she had something more important to contemplate. He had never said he didn't want to get married. He had never expressed uneasiness or fear about being a husband. And the baby, the reason for the marriage, was at first greeted with a slight trepidation, but then with anticipation. She was convinced that he wasn't necessarily ready to be a father, but was any father? He was happy. He didn't want to help with wedding arrangements or baby showers or anything smacking of 'womenfolk' stuff, but he was happy for her to organize things. He took her to his mother's house and introduced her to his mom and sister. He gave her names of friends who might come to the wedding, although none of his male friends RSVP'ed. Wait, why was that? Was it because they all knew he would do a bunk and not even be there? On the other hand, young unattached men do not like pink and white bows and flowers, champagne punch and sweet cake. Give up a Saturday night at the bars and honky-tonks? No, it wasn't an event that would have interested his friends. She hadn't been surprised that none came. It was a very small group that had gathered that Saturday night.

Another answer was that he was doing just like his father did, as his mother had indicated. 'Just leaving' was a family trait. However, what she had learned about Frankie and Old Man Monroe made her doubt some of this answer. First of all, there was no shared 'DNA'. He wasn't in the picture for most of Frankie's life. How can you model yourself on a man you don't know? Even if he did have a vision of an irresponsible father, was that enough for him to leave like that? She thought she had known him well enough to know that if he didn't want to get married, or be a father, that he would have said so.

Very sat back in the chair and stared at the ceiling. The day she had told Frankie she was pregnant, she had carefully prepared the words. He was silent while she spoke. She said she was pregnant, and that they had a couple of options. The first one she suggested was to get married, although they hadn't talked about that so soon in their relationship. She let that hang in the air for five seconds and was about to go on with the list of options when Frankie said, "Yeah, why not?" He had smiled. They never discussed the other options. It wasn't what they had planned on, but then, history was strewn with 'got pregnant and got married' couples that this wasn't out of the ordinary. And the idea of 'the sooner the better' had appealed to both.

No, she was less than certain that he hadn't imitated his father by running out. But what did happen? Where was he now? Not that she wanted him back, but now she wanted to know.

Very moved the table back from the old book case that her mother had used to stash old greeting cards, out of date coupons, magazines from last year and an entire decade of calendars. She rummaged until she found a copy of the yellow pages from some previous year. It was smaller than the ones she had remembered, but now, everyone just used the internet. She flipped through the pages until she found what she wanted and then carefully copied down the address.

She made herself a small sandwich, ate it in three bites, drank some water and refilled her water bottle. She slipped out of her flip-flops and put on a pair of sandals, wiped some lipstick across her face, grabbed her car keys and purse and headed to the carport.

Carefully, she placed the piece of paper with the address on the front seat, next to her purse. She slowly backed out of the driveway onto the curve of the street. The builders and designers had not thought that the curving narrow street, with cars parked on both sides, could have been anything but picturesque, quaint, and country-like. The reality was that it was dangerous. Backing into a street that she could not see up or down was a daily cringe for her. She had never had an accident, but she put that down to being slow, careful, and most of all, lucky. She headed downtown.

Twenty-fourth Street was crowded, and it was only two in the afternoon. The idea of widening the street had been a fifty-year battle. The businesses, and especially the residents of the Westchester neighborhood, had been fighting for as long as she could remember. The two streets of 23rd and 24th had been made one-way, lights had been installed, they had been carefully timed at 35mph. But none of this had made the traffic go more smoothly or go away. Lawsuits ensued. Everyone wanted their interests to take precedence. Noise, pedestrians, ease of traffic, all were fighting for use of the streets built for a small town and now at the heart of a city.

She turned left on Chester Avenue and headed south. It should have been 'J' street, but the desire to honor ancient city fathers prevailed for this street only. She passed stores from her childhood. The Guarantee Shoe Center was still her favorite place for shoes, and Vest's still sat on the corner of 19th, although the benches out front had gone and bars covered the windows. As she drove slowly past, she saw herself sitting on those hard, wooden benches as she had waited for her bus home. Now the bus station was further up the street and was the favored hang-out for the growing population of homeless. She saw the big block of a building that had been Brock's Department Store. She, and hundreds of other Girl and Boy Scouts, had bought Scout uniforms there. She had lunch with Great Aunt Susan in the café, visited Santa Claus in the front window.

Very turned onto 17th street and looked for the building numbers and a parking space. It was metered here, but close to her destination. She found a space and carefully parallel parked. It had been years since she had to do that, but she had remembered. She thought that learning to ride a bicycle and parallel parking had a lot in common. Once learned and practiced, the concept was never forgotten.

The modest two-story building had a single front door. She entered, her feet sticking slightly to the scuffed and dirty linoleum floor. She glanced at the list of tenants, their names and suite numbers behind a glass cabinet in interchangeable white letters. She mounted the stairs to the second floor. Ahead was a corridor, but directly in front of her was a door with gold stenciling. She knocked, entered and her shoulder briefly brushed against the sign, "Darrell Pitts – Private Investigator".

Bridget O'Shaughnessy in the guise of Miss Wonderly as she entered Sam Spade's office.

Chapter Ten: Answering Some Questions

Very encountered a very un-Sam Spade like private eye. He wore thick horn-rimmed glasses, and thin mousy hair performed a comb-over a spreading bald spot. Instead of a snappy suit, he wore khakis with a much-worn button-down shirt and no tie. This was Bako after all. He sat in front of a computer. This was the twenty-first century after all.

When Very entered, he swung his chair around and with a startled squeak said, "Hello."

"Hi. I'm hoping you can help me. I'm 37 years too late, but I'm looking for someone."

"Have a seat." He indicated a shabby, stained waiting room chair. The faux leather had peeled and split, and brownish stuffing strained to escape. Very bit her lip and willed herself not to wipe the chair. Instead she opted for a brief swipe at her own pants. How was that going to help? She sat gingerly.

"Yes, Ms…?"

"Vermilion Blew. You can call me Very."

"And who might you be looking for 37 years too late? No, don't tell me, let me guess. The man who jilted you at the altar? Or maybe, your…"

Very stood in righteous anger. "Look, I came here in good faith. I am not making fun of you, all alone in this, this, shabby little office…"

"Look, I'm sorry, that was a bad joke. I'm really sorry. I had no business saying that. Please sit down. I am a very serious business man and that was out of order. Totally out of order. Please." He indicated the shabby chair.

She huffed the huff of one who forgives a bad joke, but does not forget. She looked at the sad chair and reseated herself.

Silence enveloped the room. The computer 'binged' and the two sat waiting for the bad air to dissipate. It was like a winter morning with tule fog; the only thing to do was to wait it out until the sun strained to assert itself just about mid-morning. Bakersfieldians had learned how to wait.

Very spoke softly. "How did you know? Or was it just a lucky guess? I know I'm not alone in the 'left at the altar' scenario, but do we all come looking all these years later?"

"Given your age, it's not likely to be your birth mother. Even you must know that would be a long shot. Ditto your father. Brothers and sisters don't hold such a long-term clutch at our hearts. But sweethearts do. If it were an old boyfriend, you could probably go back to your high school or college friends and acquaintances and follow up. You wouldn't be willing to spend good money for something like that. But someone who jilted you, that might do it. But why now?"

Very slowly told the story, starting with the article in the newspaper. She was methodical, introducing a topic, and then filling in. She noted that Darrell had taken out a notebook after the first minute and was writing everything down. Soon he was interrupting and asking for spellings of names and exact dates. Very warmed to his interest and began to tell him details, adding descriptions and evaluations of the main characters. She ended her tale with the thoughts she had this morning upon learning the body was not that of Frankie Monroe, but of Daniel Harger.

When she finished, a silence again filled the office. Very could hear the hum of traffic outside and a siren in the distance.

"And so, you want to find him?" Darrell put down his pencil and looked directly into Very's face.

"Yes."

"Are you sure?"

"Yes."

"Why?"

Very hesitated. Wasn't it obvious? She had just had a scare. New information. It had upset her and opened a can of worms. Retirement, her mother's death, all of these things had fed into an emotional turmoil that demanded answers.

"When I thought he was dead, a lot of things came to the surface. I thought I was finally going to be done with it all. All of it. A cleansing, a new beginning. Sorry he was dead perhaps, but at least I was free. Now, I have realized that this was always a niggling thought in the back of my head. Where is he? Why did he leave? Would he ever come back? What did I think of it all? Now, I want to bury it, him, the whole sorry story. I want to know where he is.

Six feet under, married with children and grandchildren, whatever, I just want to know. I. Want. To. Know."

Darrell leaned back in his chair, creating a protesting squeak. "Fair enough." He again looked at her directly. "You're a librarian?"

"Yeah."

"You know how to do research?"

"Of course."

"You retired? Got some time on your hands?"

"Yes. And the point of these questions is…?"

"Do it yourself."

"What? I came here to pay you to do it. If you don't want to, just say so. If you're too busy, just say so. Why fool around with me like this?"

"No, no, you misunderstand me. I could do it, that's not a problem. It's just that, as I see it, you would be better off doing it yourself. You need to do this, that's for certain. You need to find Mr. Monroe. But I think the looking is the point, not necessarily the finding. Am I right?" Darrell looked at her with a concerned and empathetic visage.

Very stared back, meeting his gaze. "I don't know where to begin, that's why I came here."

"Okay, five-minute lesson. What you want to do is called skip tracing. We usually do this on runaway teenagers, men who try to get out of child support and so forth." Darrell rattled on for three minutes, outlining the process, the parameters and the tools. He turned to his computer and showed her how some of the research went. Very followed it all easily. "End of lesson." He pushed away from the computer and looked at Very. "Any questions?"

Very, taken by surprise, shook her head.

"Here, your homework. Come back when you're finished." He pulled a book from a small bookshelf over his head. 'The Complete Idiot's Guide to Private Investigating' was thrust into her lap. "It's a bit out of date, but still, it'll give you the basics."

Very took the book and flipped through the pages. Some pages had careful marginal notes in pencil, but otherwise the book was clean and in good shape. It wasn't Darrell who had needed the notes, but maybe it had been done for someone else? "I won't make any more notes on the pages, I'll use a pad if I need to note anything down," Very said with a wry twist of her lips.

"Hey, it's my book, I can make notes in it if I want. Sorry it's outdated, things change very quickly in my world. Laws change, computer programs change, but that will give you all the beginner's know-how needed."

"Thanks, I guess. Why are you so sure this is what I need?" Very looked directly at Darrell again.

He laughed, a throaty chuckle. "Any person who can use the word 'niggle' spontaneously, correctly, and appropriately earns my respect. I could just take your money, but you are way too smart for that. And it is obvious that you need something to do. And then, maybe you might be looking for a part time job later?"

"No, I think now I have enough to do." She turned the book over in her hands, feeling the heft of it.

"You said that the reason you thought the dead man in the orchard was your fiancé was because of the movie ticket. But it wasn't his movie ticket, obviously. Or maybe it was. What do you know about this Daniel Harger? Who was he? What was his relationship to Frankie Monroe?"

"I have never heard of him. I don't know if there is any relationship at all. If he disappeared at the same time as Frankie, maybe there is a connection. I had thought of that. I thought that maybe Frankie had been murdered too. And buried in the same orchard. Or that Frankie was… the one…"

"Who murdered Daniel Harger?"

"Yeah, I thought of that. I didn't know Frankie very long, or perhaps very well, but I truly do not believe he was a man capable of murder like that. Burying a body in a field, taking his identification. That ticket stub was so small, it must have been overlooked. No other identification was there." Very sat quietly, thinking.

"So maybe you should start with finding out about Daniel Harger. Let's see. Who supplied the dental records etc.? Family? Okay, start with wife."

Very watched Darrell type in the names and the internet pop up with names and links. Within two minutes, he said, "Bingo."

He copied a name, address and phone number onto a small piece of paper and handed it to Very. "Probably the wife. Lives in Tehachapi. Most people who have loved ones run or disappear don't move too far away. They want to stay in the area in case the missing person comes looking for them. Perhaps there were relatives to help, stay close to. And kids, you want to give your kids grandparents, even if they don't have a dad."

"I can see that you are a very good detective." Very smiled at Darrell as she used her best 'encouraging' teacher voice.

Darrell hung his head and she noticed that he blushed. His combed over bald spot turned a very deep shade of crimson.

Trying to break the awkward pause, Very took the small paper and rattled it. "Are you sure this is the wife?"

"Same last name," he muttered. "Could be a sister, mother, a cousin. But family is family and they would know each other, wouldn't they? I think that is a good place to start."

"But wouldn't she remarry? Change her name?"

"Could have done. But do you know how difficult it is to have someone declared dead? Lawyers, courts, waiting seven years? And we don't know that they had any idea he was dead. Could have just had a fight with his wife and took off. The missing person's reports don't always carry much weight unless there is a real possibility that the person is dead. Unless there was money to be gotten, most people just don't bother. Find a new man, or woman and move. Tell the neighbors you're married and bingo, no one cares."

"I suppose that makes sense. I didn't even push for a missing person's report. And neither did his mother, so as far as the law is concerned, he is still out there." Very sighed. She felt naïve, coming here with such a simple request, at least to this experienced PI. "How long will it take to find him?"

"That's why I said you could do it yourself. Couple of hours, probably. Go home, read the book."

Very laughed and stood up. "I used to say that all the time. The kids would come to me with all kinds of questions. Actually, I believe the major duty of a librarian is to teach people to look for themselves. So, I would start with the question and I would lead the kids around to the reference books, the card catalog, and then send them to the shelves to find what they were looking for. And then I'd say, 'Go home and read the book.'"

Chapter Eleven: The Dead Man's Wife

Very woke with the light. Not far above the horizon, the sun became a white disk and spread the heat and the brightness that heralded a hot dry day in the southern San Joaquin Valley. Very sighed and looked at the book by her bedside. She had not read the whole book about becoming a private investigator yesterday, but enough of it to understand the task ahead of her. She needed some time to digest the contents before she could continue.

She made coffee and toast, cut up an apple and went outside to the patio. She waited until she determined it was a decent hour to make a telephone call. She called the number Darrell had given her. The dead man's wife's phone number.

She listened for the rings and when a soft woman's voice answered, Very said, "Good morning. Is this Mrs. Ruth Harger?"

"Yes," she answered cautiously.

"Listen, I'm not a journalist, not a cop, just a person who wants to talk to you. It's very important." Very paused for any reaction from the voice, but she said nothing.

"Will you be at home this morning?" Very pressed.

"Yes."

"Okay, great. I'll be there in about an hour. Is that okay? My name is Very. Bye now." Very hung up. She slumped in her chair, sipping the last of her coffee. Was this a good idea or not? If she had a name, she needed to check it out. And she had nothing else to do, besides trolling through her mother's junk. This was a better idea.

It was a smooth drive up the hills to Tehachapi. When she drove this way as a child, there was only one lane in each direction, and it seemed to take forever. She often got car sick, but this wasn't a gut-churning bad road, and she usually managed to keep her breakfast down.

Now the road was wider, gently curving up the steep slopes. Trucks hogged the right lane and occasionally pulled out to pass, causing the passenger traffic to back up. There were too many people in too much of a hurry. Did she think this way now that she was retired and had more time to take on this trip? In 'The Grapes of Wrath,' the Joads had come this way in their escape from the Dust Bowl. They stopped and looked down on the Valley. Verdant green, it represented their future; it was to be their new home. What a joke on them. Now, if a person stopped and looked down into the Valley, all they would see was the dust, the haze, the smog, the most polluted air in the country. It used to be that a trip into the LA basin would reveal the brown smog of too many millions of cars, trucks, and factories spewing waste products. But since Los Angeles and the state of California had become alarmed and cracked down on the pollution emitters, the experience had been reversed. Now Angelenos balked at coming down into the valley from the Grapevine and being threatened by baaaaad air. What would the Joads have thought of that?

She pulled out of the haze and into the cleaner air of Tehachapi. It might have been better for the Joads to have stopped here, in the bucolic environs of the small city. Only it wasn't a city in those days; it was a wide spot in the road, a train stop on the way to the East. Now, it had begun to sprawl in all directions, with developer's neighborhoods with names of trees, birds and animals that had never lived in these hills. But they sounded good; they read like a list of upper-class dwellings and suburbs in the places where the developers had come from.

She headed for the older part of town, an address on East D Street. She slowly drove along streets that proclaimed their status as middle-class, small-town, and a tad down-at-heel. Although the houses were obviously not built as 'ticky-tacky all the same,' they had a style that proclaimed them built to the simple standard of a family house: two bedrooms, one bath and room to expand as needed. Cars dotted the streets, parked in driveways and some even on the lawns. Few were new; at least half of them were trucks or vans.

Very parked and sat in her car, contemplating the house across the street. Although the landscape appeared flat, this house had a slight rise from the cracked sidewalk to the front door. A narrow driveway ran alongside the house, disappearing into the bowels of the back yard. The front yard had two leafy trees, bushes that hugged the front wall, but whacked off at their tops to allow viewing out the front window. The multi-paned front window gave a fine view of the interior, she was sure of that. These windows were designed to show off one's Christmas tree, quality furniture, and crowded cocktail parties in the living room. But no one she knew opened their drapes any more. Who wanted their neighbors to see what was happening inside? The living room sofas that gradually faded and became worn at the edges with cat claw sharpening, wiped clean too many times of children's ice cream cone drips and a decade's worth of scattered magazines on the ring-stained coffee tables were not the stuff one wanted to show off. Best to leave the front curtains drawn and hide the detritus of one's life.

Very looked at herself in the rear-view mirror. Do not judge. Your house looks old and faded too. She looked old and faded. Since retirement she rarely put on make-up and often even forgot a dash of lipstick. Lines ran from the corners of her eyes and her lips had fine indentations that caused her lipstick to bleed into them. Age had stealthily attacked.

Very got out of her car, walked across the street and up the walkway to the front door. As she raised her hand to knock, she hesitated. She might have given Mrs. Harper some time to prepare. Maybe she wasn't up to talking about her husband's disappearance and death just yet. This was abrupt of her, to demand information today, now. There was no noise from within.

She knocked. Maybe she should have rung the doorbell? The little white nipple set into a faded black ring of Bakelite looked as though it might not work. She knocked again, a little louder this time. She put her ear closer to the door and heard the 'clop, clop, clop' of slippered feet across the floor. She heard the 'snik' of the lock opening. The door creaked on its hinges as it opened. A short woman, stooped by age or illness, peered out. Her moist eyes were ringed with red and a strained voice said, "Yes?"

"Hi, I'm Very, I called."

"Are you from the cops?" The voice was a little stronger now; the speaker surer of her ground.

"No, I'm not from the sheriff's office."

"They called yesterday. I couldn't figure out what they wanted from me."

Silence gripped the space between the women.

Very broke the impasse. "I just need to find out some information. Maybe if you let me in, we can sit down and talk?"

"My daughter isn't here."

"Oh, I thought you were Ruth Harger, Daniel Harger's wife, or rather widow, I guess."

"Yeah, you got that right."

"It's you I want to talk with, because I'm looking." She waited for Ruth to ask what she was looking for, or some other indication that she would be receptive to her visit.

The door opened wider, the old woman stepped back and with a nod, invited Very in. It was dark inside the house, as if no one had turned on a light, or bothered to open any blinds or drapes. Ruth Harger took three steps and lowered herself gently onto the end of the couch. She took a deep rattling breath and coughed.

Very suddenly realized that this woman was years older than she. She had the impression that Daniel Harger had been young, like her and Frankie, but he must have been middle-aged to have been married to this woman who was so obviously old and ill. She must be on her last legs.

Ruth Harger reached up to brush the hair out of her eyes. It was mottled brown, not gray like she had expected. Perhaps she was younger than she appeared. Not old, just ill? Ruth slowly extended her hand to a matching arm chair next to the sofa. "Sit down...please."

Very sat on the proffered chair. She looked around the room. The furniture was worn, but of reasonably good quality. Sofa, matching arm chair, two straight backed chairs that looked antique, or antiqued, and a large TV placed exactly opposite the end of the couch where Ruth Harger sat. Very could see a small dining area with a square table, piled high on one end with newspapers and old begging-for-money mail that hadn't yet found its way into the round file. Two cleared spaces were left for eating. An open door let into a small kitchen, crowded with cupboards and appliances. At the opposite end of the living room was another doorway that led into a hallway. Bedrooms and a bathroom lay beyond. Not poverty stricken, but could use more money to renovate, upgrade and maybe move to a more prestigious part of town? Stop. Who was she thinking of, herself or this newly found widow?

They sat looking at each other; Mrs. Harger with suspicion, Very with an eye to figuring out what she wanted to ask and how to ask it. This woman was not the one she had expected. Very stared at her face as she turned. Very looked into her eyes. If she pretended to have one of those computer programs that alters a person's face, what would she have looked like 37 years ago? Obviously, she was not gray and wrinkled like she was now, but was she young like Very, or more mature? What did that face look like then?

Very's mind raced on. Then, she began to feel the dizziness come over her. She had succumbed to this awful invasion of her mind with disconcerting fogginess a number of times in the last few days. What was causing it? Why did she suddenly feel dizzy when she read the paper on that fateful morning, just days ago? She didn't believe in ghosts or the paranormal, so she discounted that. She had often had premonitions; but in retrospect, awards, a slap on the wrist or meeting someone interesting were to be expected. What was her subconscious telling her now?

Very struggled to keep upright, sitting in the chair. She looked at Ruth Harger and tried not to faint. Erase the lines on Ruth's face made from years of living in a dry climate, and make her brown hair browner, fuller and in the hairstyle of 1973. Place this face on a woman who sat in the same row that she and Frankie had sat in at the Nile Theater that night. If she had known then it was the last time she would see Frankie, she would have paid more attention to him, to the surroundings and to the people sitting nearby. Now those mental pictures were hard to create from an inattentive mind. She should have paid more attention then, not let her mind wander, worry, writhe, wince and irritate her with details of her upcoming wedding. The wedding was more important to her then, but maybe, she should have been paying more attention to the other moviegoers.

Had Ruth Harger been at the Nile Theater that night? That last night before the wedding, the last night she had ever seen Frankie Monroe? And the face of a much younger Ruth Harger swirled into her brain even as the dizziness overcame her.

Chapter Twelve: Babe Harger

Very put her head down, resting on her knees. The dizzying roar subsided enough for Very to know that she would not faint, but still she hovered over her knees.

"Would you like some ice tea, sweet tea? You look like you need it." Ruth Harger heaved herself to her feet and Very listened as the older woman shuffled to the kitchen. She heard the fridge door open and the clink of ice in a glass. Soon the clink, clink of the glass returned to the living room. She heard the clunk of the glass on the coffee table in front of her.

She should have been the one to fetch refreshments. The old woman looked too old and feeble to be serving her guest anything.

"I always make it sweet, just like my mother. I don't know any other way and I can't change now. Hope it's okay." She paused then, settling herself on the couch. "Are you feeling better now?"

"Yes," Very croaked. She cleared her throat, "This is great. So nice of you. I didn't mean to impose on you."

"Nah, the tea's always there."

Very sipped some of the extremely sweet iced tea. She didn't particularly like it this sweet, but it was exactly what her mind and body craved. Need to keep her wits about herself. "This is perfect. Thanks."

Very sipped some more, then turned to Ruth. "Tell me about your husband."

"Oh, you want to know about him? It was so long ago. Well, we were married for a little over a year and I was eight months pregnant. And then he just walked away. Never looked back. I thought he was scared, about the baby, you know. But it might have been anything. I guess I have to rethink it all now. Now that they found him."

"Through the movie ticket in the pocket?" Very asked.

"Gosh, I don't really remember that, the movie. You know, with the baby. I just don't remember a lot from that time. I was all into the baby, you know how your mind gets when you are expecting? Just everything is about your baby and your own body…"

Should she interject anything about her own short, unhappy experience with being pregnant? But then, this wasn't her story to tell. She needed to listen some more. "Ummm," she affirmed.

"And I practically went into labor right after he left. And for a few weeks, it didn't matter where he was. And then I had my baby. I didn't get around to filing a missing person's report until later, much later. I was too busy, way too busy. With a baby, alone. Well, not alone, my folks were around. But I don't think that Danny would have been much of a dad in any case. He wasn't around all the time."

"But they identified that body, presumably it had been there for 37 years. But they did it rather quickly, don't you think?" Very said.

"When I filed the missing person's report, they asked me if he had been to a dentist and he had. They gave the records they had, dental records, they called them. And that was part of the file. Who would have thought that they would have gone back all those years and found his dentist's x-rays and stuff? All those years?"

Very looked at Ruth, now stronger and livelier than she had a few minutes before. Talking about 'Danny' seemed to have revived her.

"I think that we need to give credit to the Sheriff's Department. This was a 'cold case' I'm sure. They must have been very thorough. I am impressed with them." Very mouthed the platitudes. Because neither she nor Frankie's mother had ever filed a missing person's report, their missing son/fiancé would never be looked for. Danny's body wasn't just found, but was identified quickly because someone cared. "I've heard that Kern County has a lot of dead bodies that show up. Mountains, deserts, old mine shafts, I guess we could add orchards, too. Places that are out of the way, no one goes there. So there are lots of missing persons and bodies. It's more than most places, I guess. But we do have high crime rates, so…" Very stuttered to a stop. Rattling on wasn't getting her closer to the goal she had. "Did the sheriff say how he died, did they know?"

Ruth hesitated a moment. "They said 'suspicious'. I think that means murder, doesn't it? I know they said he was buried years ago, maybe at the time of his disappearance. If he was dead and they buried him, that generally means murder, doesn't it? If you commit suicide, you don't bury yourself, do you? Someone wanted to hide the body, obviously."

"Do you know who wanted him dead?" Very gently asked.

"The cops asked that too, but I didn't say anything. Just that he disappeared."

"This sounds terrible, Ruth," Very said.

"Oh, call be Babe, everyone does. It's a nickname from childhood and it stuck. Gosh, I haven't heard anyone use Ruth lately. That is, until the cops called me. Yes, it's terrible, to think he was murdered. And I can't think of anyone who wanted him dead. Sometimes I did, but, never mind about that now."

"Let's talk about happier times," Very suggested.

"Photo," Babe muttered, "I have one here." She struggled to get up, finally falling back on the sofa. She pointed to a shelf that held books and a few photos. "That one on the end, that's me and Danny Boy. They always called me Babe and they always called him Danny Boy. You know, the old Irish song 'Danny Boy'," she warbled off key.

Very jumped up and went to the shelf. She found the photo easily. It was set in a cheap frame and the colors had washed out by being exposed to light and heat. The photographer was obviously an amateur as the lines were blurred and the pose poorly composed with light coming over their shoulders, throwing shadows on their faces. Very brought the photo back to the couch with her and held it between them as she sat down.

"Yeah, Babe and Danny Boy. It's been sitting on a shelf in my house since it was taken. My daughter grew up with her dad watching over her. If she did something bad, I'd point to this photo and say, 'Better be careful, your dad will have something to say about this.'" She chuckled. "I never said where he'd gone, 'cause I didn't know. But I tried to make him here, watching his little girl grow up. That isn't a bad thing, is it? I tried to give her something she couldn't have. I tried to make her feel loved. Or at least make her feel he cared. I would say things like, 'Your dad would be really proud of you' too, not just bad stuff. Ah Danny Boy." She touched the photo, stroking his face.

Very watched as Babe held the photo. She also looked at the couple. She could see the younger Babe in the older woman beside her. She squinted at Danny Boy Harger and tried to picture him as the man he would be now. He'd be gray-haired, probably with a lot less hair as she could see the receding hairline even in this youthful photo. She imagined deep lines running on either side of his mouth down to his chin, crows' feet radiating from those dark eyes. He would still be slender, more wiry and feisty than fat, and contented. She leaned over to get a better look and she felt it again, the dizziness. Very leaned back into her own chair and breathed deeply. Get a grip, have her little dizzy spell another time.

"And all those years, you waited for him? Did you look for him?" Very pressed on, over her own feelings of unease and faintness.

"Oh, I just got on with life. At first, I thought he would come back. My folks were just down the street, helped me out with the mortgage on this house, babysat for Cassandra when I went to work. They were the ones that made me finally file the missing person's report. My dad went with me and worked on the dentist stuff. But it didn't find him then, did it?" She sighed.

"That dental report helped identify him now," Very pointed out.

"Fat lot of good it does now, huh?"

"Did you ever have him declared dead? Or did you feel as though he were out there and would come back?" Very's voice was off-hand and she hoped just vaguely curious. She didn't want to seem to be grilling Babe.

"Oh yeah, my Dad helped with that too. But they wanted all kinds of things at Social Security. Not that there was going to be much money from that angle. But they wanted all kinds of information about employers and addresses and what not. He didn't have any insurance and he didn't really work much, at least on-the-books kind. So, it was just too much trouble. They also wanted to know about his family. But I couldn't tell them much. I told my dad to not bother. I supported myself and my girl. I was a hairdresser for a while and I also clerked at the local five and dime. When my Cassandra got older, she would find little jobs here and there, babysitting, that sort of thing. We got along great and she earned her own pocket money. She didn't mind, it was good for her. We didn't need any Social Security money and frankly, we didn't need him. We got along fine. We did great."

Very sat back in her chair and tried to figure out what Babe meant exactly by all her ramblings.

"Why are you here? Why do you care all about this?" Babe turned to face Very.

Very tried to place a mask on her face, tried to look neutral and independent. She had been expecting this question, but hadn't yet gotten her answer straight. She took a deep breath without looking as though she were gearing up to tell something other than the truth.

"It's just that I thought your husband, your late, very late husband was my fiancé. But it wasn't, so I thought that there might have been a connection. I just wanted to know how your man went missing. Maybe there was a connection, you know. That movie ticket in his pocket was just so unusual, so specific. We went to the movies together that night. That was the last time I saw him. We were going to be married the next day. It was all planned and everyone was there and then… He didn't show up. No one had seen him, no one knew where he was. I, I just didn't know what to think. His mother said that he had run away, backed out. She said it was a family trait, to run away from things. So, I just left it at that. But when they found the body in the orchard and there was that ticket in the pocket, I just knew that it was him. But it wasn't. So, now I'm looking to see what happened to him. Maybe your husband knew him? Maybe he knew something, or maybe you knew something. So, I am here looking for information."

"Who was your fiancé?" Babe demanded.

"Frankie, Frankie Monroe. Did Danny know him?" Very leaned forward and listened for Babe's answer.

Babe's eyes slid sideways. Then she raised her head and looked directly at Very. Now her eyes were wide open. "Never heard of him. I don't know no Frankie Monroe. No, no friend of Danny's." Her head fell back onto her chest and she fumbled with the top button of her faded and stained sweater. "I'm sorry, I'm not well. I don't have much to tell you. Sorry about that."

Very could see that Babe was tired and not well. But she had come a long way to talk with her and she couldn't just leave now. Now that she knew she was lying. She knew the symptoms and Babe Harger knew more than she was telling.

Chapter Thirteen: Danny Boy's Friends

"Well, could you tell me about his other friends? Maybe we can help each other?" Very leaned in close and spoke quietly to Babe, willing her to perk up and keep talking.

Babe seemed to recover slightly, but was obviously tiring.

"Maybe I can get you some tea? Would you like some sweet tea? I'll go get it for you; you just stay there and rest." Very jumped up before Babe could answer and whisked off to the kitchen. The plastic tea container had never made it back to the icebox door, so Very quietly searched for the glasses and then poured a similar glass of tea for Babe. She found some ice cubes and slipped them in. She tiptoed back into the living room.

When she got back from the kitchen, she saw that Babe had risen from her place on the couch and had gone to the tall cabinet where the photograph had been placed. Drawers and cupboards held family mementoes that debouched now onto the floor. Babe held an old cigar box in her hands. It was made of wood and the paper that covered it revealed the brand name. It was a sturdy old box that had weathered years of collections and numerous openings and closings. Babe had turned her back and was rifling through the contents.

"Here, I've brought you some tea. I'll put it on the coffee table." Very looked around for a coaster, and found none. There were hundreds of faint round stains on the old wooden coffee table top. She placed the glass directly on the table and watched condensation form on the outside. Within a minute, this glass too would be adding one more ring. One more among hundreds wouldn't make any difference now.

Babe slowly walked back to the couch and gingerly seated herself, the box on her lap. "Hey, I've found a photo you might be interested in. You know, I'm not from here, but Danny went to high school here, in Oildale. He was friendly with a lot of people. Some of them I didn't like. Some were just leftovers from a time before he met me. He just kept being friends with them, but I let him know that I didn't like them and didn't want to hang around with them. But I kept a few photos. If you're looking, you might look at these. Or really, this one." She passed a photo to Very. It was a snapshot, slightly out of focus, of three young men. It screamed the 70's. They wore their hair long, that 70's style with sideburns or a mustache, or both. The shirts were bright with flowers and stripes. They grinned stupidly like they were high on drugs.

Very stood and took the photo to the window to get a better look. There was Danny, looking much as he had in the other photo that Babe had shown her. And then, two other young men. Very didn't recognize either of them. Presumably they also lived and went to school in Oildale, so Very wouldn't have known them, if they were the same age as she.

Babe had said that if Very were looking, she should see these. What was Very looking for? Danny was dead, she said that she didn't know Frankie, so what did she think showing her these photos could help with? Looking for Frankie? So, why was she showing Very these photos? Was she trying to build on the lie that Very knew she had been told? To throw Very off the scent, off the track?

"Am I looking for something?" Very asked. "Will this tell me something more? About my Frankie? Or is this about Danny?"

Babe took the photo back and started to ramble. "So here is Q-Ball. I know that it looks like he has hair, but he doesn't have much. He had that bald spot in the back and the stuff in his eyes really comes from the side. If he cut his hair, like they used to, before this, he was bald, like a billiard ball, like a baby. So they named him Q-Ball like the ball that you use to line up the other balls. It's white and bald. But they spelled it with a 'Q'. So, that's one. And then there is Curly. Look at that hair!" Babe pointed to one of the boys whose face was almost hidden by clouds of blond curls. "And here is Danny, long hair too, but not as bad as the others. Don't have a picture of Killer, one of the others. Look at Danny! Danny Boy was always a boy, so young, so immature. It was easy to call him Danny Boy."

Very looked a little closer at Danny. His brown hair fell into his face and his wide grin exposed a mouthful of teeth that had never seen an orthodontist, but should have. His elfin face beamed directly into the camera, as if he knew who his audience was. She was in agreement with Babe, Danny Boy looked young and immature. "When was this taken, what year, do you know?"

"Nah, high school, or after. Look at those dreamy eyes; he got me with those dreamy eyes." Babe sighed and smiled at the photo.

This was something that Very couldn't agree with, so she remained silent, waiting for Babe to go on.

"They were in a band, you know," Babe said smugly, like a teenage bragging about her boyfriend. "They actually played gigs around town, sometimes."

"The three of them?" Very looked again and wondered what kind of music they played, loud rock music, presumably. That was the kind of music that could be played by anyone who learned a few chords on the guitar and could scream into a microphone. No musical ability needed. "Do you have any other photos? Later ones of Danny Boy, maybe?"

Babe put her head down and shuffled through the cigar box, peeking at some photos and swiftly moving past others. She shielded the contents from Very's prying eyes. "No, no, no more. Just that one. And then the one of the two of us. The rest are just baby pictures and family stuff."

"Could I take pictures of these?" Very quizzed Babe. She held up the photo of the boy's band and the one of the two of them, the wedding photo. "I'd like that. It might be helpful for me as I look." Very deliberately used the word 'look' in an attempt to bring Babe back to her own use of that word.

Babe gave her tacit consent by slamming the cigar box shut, leaving the one photo out on the table. Very dug in her purse quickly. She pulled out her new 'smart' phone. It had been a recent purchase; a leap of faith in technology and the future. Now, how to work the camera. The face of the phone showed a variety of icons, one of which looked like an old-fashioned camera. That must be the camera function. These old-fashioned icons, like phones, would youngsters recognize them in the future? She tapped on the camera icon and she could see the coffee table in front of her. She bent down to get a good shot of the three boys, filling the frame with their 40-year-old likenesses. She pushed at a button and heard a click. Hopefully, that was the camera phone taking a photo. The 'click' wasn't necessary with the digital camera, as there was no mirror snapping back into place, but it was reassuring to know that she had probably taken the photo. She bent closer and took another. Then she moved the photo of the two love birds closer. The light from the window made a glare on the glass. She moved it and the glare disappeared, but the absence of light made the photo darker. Never mind, it was what it was. She took three of this one.

Very leaned back into her seat and then noticed Babe. She clutched the wooden box tightly on her lap, her head resting on the back of the couch, her mouth open, her skin pale, almost translucent in patches. She looked very old, and ill. Very waited before disturbing her, letting her rest.

Eventually, Babe opened her eyes. Watery eyes stared at Very; incomprehension clouded Babe's face. "Who? What?"

"Babe, thanks for the photos. I appreciate them," Very said slowly and distinctly, trying not to startle or agitate her.

"You can't have them. You can't have these." Babe's thin unsteady hands gripped the box.

"It's okay, I'm not taking anything," she responded, trying not to remind Babe that she was indeed taking something away, the images on her camera phone.

"I just wanted to know one more thing. Are you planning to have a funeral? Sometime?" Very said gently.

"Funeral, who needs a funeral? I'm not dead yet. No, no, no. You're not pushing me into my grave yet, girlie. Who do you think you are? Get out of here! Where are my pictures? What are you doing with my pictures?"

"Here they are," Very said, pushing the one of the three boys towards Babe.

Babe snatched at it and swiftly shoved it into the box, slamming the lid so that the sound echoed in the room.

"And here's this one," Very offered the framed photo of the lovebirds.

Babe looked at it in Very's proffered hand. Her right hand came away from the box and with surprising strength, quickly smacked the frame out of Very's hand, sending it flying across the room. Very heard it land on the floor, but did not hear the sound of breaking glass. "Pile of shit. Pile of shit." She looked at where the photo had landed and breathed heavily. "You pile of shit!"

"I think it's time for me to go. Is there anything I can do for you?" Very waited only a heartbeat for an answer before she stood and headed for the door. "I'll see myself out. Nice to meet you."

Very smiled in Babe's direction. Babe sat in her place on the couch, breathing noisily and heavily. She made no attempt to acknowledge Very's comments or her impending departure.

"Bye, and thank you," said Very as she slipped out the door. She hoped Babe would lock it behind her, but feared she wouldn't remember to do that.

Very crossed the street, looking both ways. She needn't have bothered as no traffic was visible or audible. She slipped into the front seat and settled herself. She looked at her phone, but couldn't find where her photos might be. Which icon kept her just-taken photos? A photo album icon? What would that look like? New technology, but also new tricks. She sighed.

She pulled out a small notebook that she had placed in her purse as she had left the house. The 'Complete Idiot's Guide' had told her to make notes as she went along, so she wouldn't forget. Now, she dutifully wrote down where and when and who. What had she learned? Danny Boy Harger had a band and two friends that played with him. Where were Q-Ball and Curly now? Could they tell her anything? She had the photos and she knew they had all gone to high school, in Oildale. She knew the approximate date of Babe and Danny's wedding and that there had been a child, a daughter.

What else? She knew that Babe Harger was ill, physically and perhaps mentally as well. She had spoken warmly of him, of her husband who had disappeared. She kept a photo of the two of them on a cabinet shelf. Had she loved him? He had given her a daughter, and there were some photos of her on the cabinet as well; Very had glimpsed a number of childhood photos. But what had she really thought of him? The last comment she had made of him, 'pile of shit,' seemed to be more thoughtful and truthful than any other. Or was it anger suddenly coming out? You could love and hate someone at the same time, she knew from experience. You could hate the disappearing act, but you could still cling to the good times.

Good times. With Frankie? But what about the lie, about knowing Frankie? Babe's lie lay there. What did it mean?

Chapter Fourteen: The PI's Office

It was only 11:30 when Very arrived back at Darrell's office. She burst into his office as she had the day before, barely knocking on the door as she had her hand on the knob. As before, she found Darrell seated at his desk, in front of the computer screen. He turned to her with a welcoming smile. "Hello."

"Hello," Very mumbled as she threw herself into the same chair, not bothering with cleaning it.

"You've found something?" Darrell smiled more broadly.

"She's lying." Very looked at Darrell, daring him to contradict her.

"Ah, you need to tell me about your visit to the grieving widow. She was the widow, I take it?" Darrell swiveled his chair to face Very directly.

Very took a deep breath and let it whoosh out, emptying some of the anxiety out of her body. She replayed the visit, trying to remember word for word what had been asked and answered. "Oh, I should have written all of this down, not just some of it," she complained at one point.

"Never mind, next time," Darrell encouraged her.

Very tapped and turned on her phone, intending to show him the photos, but in the end, she handed it over to Darrell to find. A mini-lesson about the camera and album ensued. Together they looked at the photo of Babe and Danny at their wedding and the one of Danny and his two friends, the boys in the band. "And then I asked about Frankie Monroe. She said she knew nothing about him, but I know she was lying. I know lying. The little eye movements, the stare into your face, wide eyed and not blinking. Oh, I know them all." Very went silent.

"You need to write it all down. That way you can add and subtract later, but at least it is all there, what you heard and saw each time. Each search leaves a trace, so you can go back and see the holes, the unanswered questions. Or what questions you should have asked. Or in your case, which questions were asked and not answered truthfully."

"Ummm," answered Very. "Of course, I have a little notebook. I have half a dozen unopened, empty notebooks around my house. Gifts, from students, friends. You know the thing; what do you get a librarian, or your English teacher for her birthday, or Christmas or end-of-year gift? A fancy little notebook. My mother taught me to never throw away anything."

"Well, there you go!" Darrell smiled at her again.

"But I'm afraid I only took the briefest of notes. No time." Very couldn't help but smile back. It was human nature to return the emotional cues.

"Now, did you get started on the book I lent you?" he asked.

"I read it," came the answer, rather too quickly.

Darrell's chair clunked as it flipped back into position in surprise. "You read it all?"

"I'm a reader, remember? I didn't really read all of it, just the applicable parts. But I skimmed the other sections for ideas. But yeah, I read it."

"So, if you want to find Frankie Monroe, you need to try doing a skip search. Where do we start? What do you have?" Darrell leaned forward, as if he wanted to dig into Very's cache of knowledge, whatever was in her head, her memories, her impressions, deep into her brain to extract any morsel of information that would help.

Very shook her head, trying to shake off the feelings of unwanted penetration into her brain. He was only trying to help. He was on her side.

"I have a name, a birthdate, possibly correct. No Social Security Number. So, social media? Very unlikely. Public data bases? Maybe, if I could find his number. Death databases?"

"Where do you want to start?" Darrell asked, more neutral now, back to the businessman persona.

"Actually, let's start with lunch. It's been a long time since breakfast." Very stood, wanting to put off the next part of this search until later, until she readied herself to talk about Frankie.

"Okay, let's go to my favorite hole-in-the-wall sandwich place." Darrell smiled again, friendly, but more stand-offish than just a few minutes before.

The casual restaurant was full, but they found places at a shared table with two secretary-types. They said 'Hi' to Darrell as if they recognized him by sight, but not by name. Very had the soup and salad combo and Darrell ordered a stacked sandwich. The cheese, meat, mayo and avocado slices oozed out the sides and bottom of the roll. Sheaves of paper napkins, fingers and the heels of his hands became Darrell's weapons, trying to contain the leaking ingredients and redirecting them into his mouth.

It was not a pretty sight. The two young women looked askance at Darrell and sympathetically at Very as they took their leave.

At last, Darrell declared victory, as he pushed the remaining morsel of slippery avocado into his mouth. He emptied the metal napkin holder and carefully wiped his fingers, hands, mouth and face as he attempted to destroy the evidence of the war between Darrell and his lunch. He took his glass of mostly ice and a little cola and brought it carefully to his lips, sipping demurely as if trying to make up for the spectacle of the battle.

When Darrell appeared ready to join a conversation, Very asked in a too-bright voice, "How did you get into the PI business?"

Darrell sighed as if this was something he could do successfully. "I majored in accounting at Cal State Bakersfield. Nice, safe occupation. Always have a job, you know? I went to work for an insurance company, a small, local place. A good job. I did some investigations into insurance fraud. Looking into the books, adding the columns, checking the comings and goings of all the money. That sort of thing fascinated me. Then I did some workman's compensation claims. In the first one, the employer didn't want to pay because he thought the worker was cheating on him. I guess the company could have, and probably should have, employed a professional investigator, but they were doing it on the cheap. Let the new guy do the weird stuff. I actually did a couple of stake-outs, trying to catch people doing yard work, or driving a car when they said they couldn't. And I found I liked it, the investigating. So, a PI that the company had hired, then hired me to do some extra work for him. I showed him how this company accountant was fiddling the books. The PI liked the idea of having an accountant to do that kind of fraud work and also do his accounts. I worked with him for a couple of years, let him do the stake-outs, not really my cup of tea, actually. And then he retired. Left me out in the cold. I went back to the insurance company and they encouraged me to get my PI license, so that they could use me instead of hiring an outside person. Now, it's the other way around; I'm independent, but get a lot of my work from the insurance company. I have an associate, another independent PI, do the stake-out work. Some people like that stuff, but I don't. I like sleeping in my own bed, eating regular meals, and using proper facilities for the uh…"

"I can imagine. You don't need any details on that one. So, what do you do mostly?" Very smiled back, her encouraging teacher smile.

"Skip tracing. I'm good at it, but it can get a bit tedious and repetitive. That's why I said you might do your own." He paused a beat, waiting for a response, any response from Very.

"I've read the book, I think I could do it. But, is that what I want to do?" Very spoke to herself as much as to Darrell.

"It'll be faster. I'll only do the looking when I have time. It's not high priority for me, not like it might be for you," Darrell said simply, looking for Very's reaction.

"And if you had more time, by not taking my case, what would you do with it? What do you do with your spare time?"

"Don't laugh. Some people think it's a silly hobby, but I find it has all the right ingredients for a healthy, interesting, always changing thing to do. I'm a bird-watcher." He looked sideways at Very.

She understood his reply, his glance; he was watching for her reception to his answer. Why did he care so much about her attitude about his hobby? Was he expecting a snide comeback? Well, he wasn't going to have to defend himself from her opinion. "That's great. Do you belong to the Audubon Society?"

"Ummm," came the answer, from his lowered head.

"It's a kind of detective work, isn't it? Trying to find the birds? I guess if you put yourself in their position, try to think like a bird, you might find them more easily. If you understand their habits, their thoughts, their psychology, well, then it would be easier to discover where they would be and when, wouldn't it? Just another way of being a detective." Very spoke to the lowered head, which eventually lifted to meet her gaze.

"I never thought of it that way," he mumbled. But his eyes met hers. "Do you want me to show you how to search?" He smiled at her. "Not birds, people, I mean. I can make some time this afternoon, then you can get started."

"Well, I guess. Yeah. I don't have much else to do," she said, pushing away thoughts of closets, cupboards and boxes.

He hesitated. "Can I ask you a personal question? Just asking. How did you get your name? Very? Vermilion?"

Very sighed. The long or the short version? She inhaled and let the long version out, trying to keep the whine to a minimum. "My mother wanted a 'red' name. Other girls get named boring things like Rose, Scarlett, Ruby, Rowena, Cherry, Berry. Even Garnet, Poppy, Strawberry, Plum, Ginger, Crimson, Cinnabar, Cinnamon, or Burgundy would have been better. But no, she chose Vermilion." She snapped her mouth shut with an angry 'smack'.

"I think it's cool, different, interesting. You know you can change it? It costs money, but it's possible."

"Yeah, I know. But now I own it; it's too late."

They walked back to the office together, companionably.

"You know, the library has a history room. Well, you know that, don't you, you're a librarian. They have yearbooks. All of them. They asked for donations, once, and they got so many that they turned a lot of people away. But they were able to make a pretty complete collection. If your man, or friends of, went to school in Bakersfield, you could look there. They might give you some more ideas."

"Frankie didn't, but Danny Boy Harger did. Mmmmm." Very was silent, thinking. Darrell didn't interrupt, just walked beside her.

When they reached the office, Darrell made a place for Very to sit just behind his shoulder as he prepared to show her his files. Very took out her little notebook and mechanical pencil. Maybe she needed a larger notebook, or a completely different one, if she was going to take notes all day long.

"Can you see alright?" Darrell asked over his shoulder.

"Yeah, I can see, maybe not the little details, but I can follow. Just go slowly, so I can take notes."

"I'll start with the easy stuff. The free data bases are getting better and better and if a person hasn't left the immediate area, you can find them sooooo easily. It's when they move five states away that it can get a bit tricky. But here, this site is great." Darrell brought up a website and typed in his own name. A raft of information flew up to the screen. Very gasped at the detail on Darrell that was available to the casual flying fingers.

"Is that available on me too?" Very whispered.

"Oh yeah, and there is more." Darrell quickly moved from site to site, showing the minutiae of his life. He ran a commentary on what was there and what wasn't. Finally, he stopped. "I've now exhausted the easy stuff. There are more websites, but they have no more information on me. It's just a duplicate of this. And you notice, no SSNs, no bank account numbers, no real information beyond this stuff. But this is a lot.

"Now, let's try Daniel Harger. Since he's been dead for 37 years, or thereabouts, he shouldn't be here at all."

Darrell went through the same steps he had for himself, coming up with only the name with other birthdates and obviously other Daniel Hargers. No Danny Boy Harger. Darrell talked Very through each of the steps, while Very took notes. "Now, let's look for variations. Dan, Danny." Darrell did it all over again, much faster this time as he didn't need to wait for Very to take notes. "Do we have a middle name? That might give us other clues. For example, people who want to disappear often use their middle name as a first name, or drop their last name in favor of a middle name as a last name. Or use a variation, like Danny or Dannie, or Dan or switch the first, middle and last names in some sort of new combination. The 'anagram' of murder mysteries isn't a thing in the real world. Too sophisticated for the not quite bright criminals or runaway dads. We don't want to give up our names altogether, we just want to try and hide. I'd say 95% of skip tracing revolves around some variation of a person's name. Or at least, that's my experience."

Darrell turned in his seat and looked to see if Very was still with him. She lowered her head and pretended to be writing notes as she avoided his glance. He turned back.

"So, what was the fiancé's full name? You called him 'Frankie'. So, was it Francis, Frank, Francisco, Franklin? Or maybe Franco or Frantz or Francois? We'll look up in this website for variations." Darrell clicked onto another website and found even more variations. "Or maybe he used his first name as a last name, so we can look at that. What about his middle name? Could it be used, or a variation of it, as a first name, or a last name?"

Very sighed and caused Darrell to turn in his seat. "Still want to try and find him?" he asked.

"Well, I thought I had found him, but now…"

"You must have really loved that guy!"

Mist came over her brain again. She gripped the edge of the desk and breathed deeply. Why was he saying that? Had she been in love with Frankie? What does that mean? Were they getting married because of the baby and for no other reason? She wasn't sure of any motive any more, or all of them. Which combination should she choose to believe in, now?

A glass of water appeared at her hand. Very hadn't seen or heard it being prepared; it appeared by stealth.

"Go ahead, drink it. It's good water, filtered. Not out-of-the-tap Bakersfield water." Darrell pressed it closer to her closed fist. "Don't faint on me. Drink the water." He leaned a little closer.

Very took a deep breath. Return to the present, leave 1973 behind.

Chapter Fifteen: The Library History Room

After Very recovered, Darrell suggested that she needed to check out the Library, specifically the History Room. "It's a great place to do research on Bakersfield and Kern County. Often, I'm contacted by someone outside who needs some legwork done on this area. You'd be surprised at the number of people who leave this town. Graduate from school and go somewhere else, never to return. So, the Library has a special room with nothing but old documents from Kern county. I think you need to go there and take a look at the yearbooks. They've got them all. If you don't find them in one high school, try another. It's open in the afternoons only, so this is the perfect time. Uh, if you feel up to it that is."

"Yes, I feel better now. It's just since this whole 'finding the body' business, I often become overwhelmed and feel faint. Anxiety? Stress? My blood pressure is maybe a bit high." She smiled at Darrell to reassure him that she was capable of going to the library, on her own.

A few minutes later, she found herself waiting outside the door of the History Room. Occupying the northwest corner of the ground floor, it had a large plate glass window that gave, to all those in, and all those out, a view of each other. A woman of mature years appeared and noisily produced a ring of keys. As she found the right one, she rattled them, making sure that everyone within earshot knew that she was now opening the door to the Kern County History Room. Very was the only one waiting to enter, and she appropriately stood at attention and waited for the guardian to open the gates.

The space was surprisingly small. Although Very knew about this important resource, she had never been inside the room. She entered and stood in the middle, scanning the shelves for what she wanted. Then she saw them, hundreds it looked like, crowded into shelves that lined a whole wall. Anyone who had been to high school in the county in the last 70 or 80 years, had their yearbook here, forever keeping that beguiling senior photo as fresh as the day it was taken. Very turned to the key keeper, "May I?" She gestured towards the yearbooks.

First, Very found her own and opened it. The volume had been donated by one of the lesser known figures of her class; someone who had moved away and never showed up at reunions. Probably left the book at home and his parents had been ready to throw it away. If the library wanted it, they thought, give it away, as their child was in no mood to ever look at it again. There was only one 'signature' across the face of the only other student in the class who could have been said to have been a friend. The rest of the pages were empty and the paper felt slightly tacky from the printer's ink. Never even looked at it. Had his best friend sign, then chucked it into the back of a closet. Done with high school. She wished him well, wherever he was. High school wasn't always the highlight of a teenager's life.

Very found her photo and those of a few friends. The day it was taken she combed the hair into neatness and tied a small ribbon in it to keep it off her face. The smooth 'wings' of almost shoulder length hair framed her face. No smile, and she looked into a corner, away from the camera, not into it. She did a number of poses, and this was the one she chose. Why? Less ugly? She knew she wasn't pretty, not even close, but youth and a professional photographer made her acceptable for the yearbook and a framed photo for the mantelpiece. So much prettier then.

She reshelved the book. She scanned the adjacent shelves until she found the school and the years that she thought might have some photos of the people she was looking for. She took them to a table in the middle of the room. She crowded no one, so she spread them out in front of her, including her notebook.

She started with 1966. Among the seniors, the name: Daniel Harger. Bingo. There he was, looking much as he did in the wedding photo, which was a few years later, and also similar to the 'band' photo. Shorter hair in 1966, a bit more of a baby face, but definitely the same man. Then she looked in the clubs, sports, student government, nothing. A loser, a loner? She scanned the other photos, looking for Q-Ball and Curly. If you had friends from school, they would be from the same year. Only later did kids start hanging with friends that were older or younger. Finally, among a number of random shots at the very back of the book, labeled "Danny Boy and Band," was what she was looking for. Danny, front and center, holding a guitar low on his hips while he strummed. He was flanked by his 'band' of two, Q-Ball and Curly. So, Danny, as a senior, had a band, with the two others that were in the later picture. But the two weren't here in the yearbook. Why?

How about 1965? Maybe the two, Q-Ball and Curly, were older, or younger, or dropped out of school? Very picked up 1965. She started with the junior class, finding Danny Harger again. Oh, here he was listed as Danny, not Daniel. And then she saw him, Q-Ball. He suffered from male pattern baldness at the age of 16. And he had cut the little hair that he had on the sides. Bald, like a cue ball. Stanley Leon. Very got her camera out and quickly snapped a photo. She had one already, but this was a portrait and his features were clear. Very looked through the rest of the book, trying to find any more photos. No band photo this year.

She went back to the junior class and looked harder, making sure of each boy. Searching for the facial features, the hair. Finally, she found him. His hair was the result of an attempt to tame what she knew was almost untamable. It was cut. Only an inch and a half remained of what later would be the biggest Afro on a white kid in Bakersfield. Glenn Wilson. Very took another photo. She flipped through, looking for his name among the athletes, the star intellectual students, the civic-minded prodigies, even the worker bees of the minor clubs. Nada.

Very stood and slammed the book shut. She looked at the shelf and gathered the volumes from the table in front of her.

"Never mind, I'll do that. We close in five minutes, so you can leave," the attendant said.

Very looked at the woman and nodded. "Thanks. Actually, I understand completely where you are coming from. If a book is misshelved, it's like it's lost. Better to replace it yourself than to have some person who doesn't care put it back on the shelf. I'll leave it for you."

"I'm glad you understand. I often tell someone I'll shelve it for them and they refuse. Then I have to be hawkeyed about checking before they leave that they've done it right. How hard is it to put the yearbooks in year order? You'd be surprised!"

"No, I wouldn't. I was a librarian myself, over 30 years. Retired now." Very smiled at the attendant.

"If you ever find yourself with time on your hands, we could always use some volunteer work around here. I'm sure we could find something useful for you to do. Like looking for 'lost' books."

"Hmmm, I'll think about that. I was a star at that when I was in college. However, right now, I'm hot on the trail of a missing friend. Thanks."

Very picked up her notebook and purse and then glanced up to the shelves. Bakersfield College yearbooks as well, she noted. But did any of these 'boys' go on to college, even the local community college? She tucked the information away for future reference.

It was a melancholy drive home. She had found Danny's friends, their names and presumably their ages as well. What more was she looking for? Was she disappointed in not finding Frankie as well? His mother and sister had said they had been in Redding, so presumably he had graduated from there, not here in Bakersfield. But what about BC? What about those other yearbooks with photos and friends? It was a bit of a longshot. She now had names, and more and better ways to look them up.

When she arrived home, she found her cat sitting at the back door, waiting to be let in, given her dinner and petted. Very did all that first, then heated up some leftovers for dinner. After that, she found some classical music on the Internet. Thank goodness for the Internet radio. Bakersfield had only a few hours a day of classical music, on the public radio station, so she often sought music elsewhere. She had loved the Beatles at 15, but as she grew older, her taste in music had not kept up with the times, instead it had regressed. She preferred music that was at least 100 or 300 years old now. This current stuff was not going to last the ages.

She uploaded the photos from her phone onto her own computer. Then she printed them out, enlarging and giving them the best balance of light she could get. She then took a large piece of paper and started a time line. She estimated dates of birth for all her major characters, including Frankie's mother, sister and 'Old Man Monroe.' Same with Danny Boy. She tried to get as close as possible to the real dates, at least the years. Then she put high school dates, graduation, job years, although she knew little of when and where.

Suddenly, she realized she had left out an important person, herself. Of course, she was a player in all this. If she negated herself, she wouldn't be able to see the whole picture, only the parts that she had had no control over. But had she had control over her own actions, her own role in this? Of course, the past was gone, she couldn't control that, or her actions in the past. But could she see things in a different light? Could she step out of herself and view the past with dispassion? Could she put herself on the paper as a player and just be this other player, without viewing Very as 'herself'? She put herself down, and added the timelines that seemed to be part of the patterns she saw. Immediately, she saw herself as a college student, away from Bakersfield for these four important years. She had missed all the bands, the 'happenings' and the gossip of comings and goings. Who married whom, who remained in Bakersfield and who had escaped. These were all unknowns to her. Yes, she had come home at Christmas, but she only saw her own small circle of family and friends. Summers were spent elsewhere, at camp or working in the university library, so she had become rather out of touch. When she came home from college, degree in hand, but no plans, she fell into a round of volunteer jobs, reacquainting herself with high school friends, and avoided the big problem of the 'job'. Sissy had been happy to have a temporary playmate and her father, in particular, had been happy to have her close again after the years away. Her mother tried hard to bite her tongue about what her plans were for the future. Very spent a lot of time cooking for everyone and cleaning the dishes, allowing her mother to relax and watch TV or read a book. It was a ploy to deflect what she thought of as the complaint on the tip of her mother's tongue about a grown child with a fancy, but useless, degree.

Then she met Frankie and spent most evenings and weekends with him. They had met in the backyard of a high school friend. There were a lot of people there and after a drink, she knew she had come because she wanted to meet someone new. Frankie approached her, in a shy roundabout way, and asked if she wanted something more to drink. He smiled at her and she saw no reason to say no. It was only a drink. She didn't size him up, or judge if he was 'suitable' material for a boyfriend, it was just a drink. He made her laugh, and he seemed to only have eyes for her that night. She found out that he wasn't as educated as she, but the well-educated men of the college were not very interested in a girl from Bakersfield, the boonies of California. She had seldom dated, only spending time with this one and that one, waiting for the right one to come along. Although a white horse and shining armor might have seemed desirable, she knew she'd never find them accompanying a man. Just let him be nice and interested in her.

Frankie was handsome. But if she stepped away, she would have said his face was too broad, his nose too snubbed, his hair too wild and unruly, his teeth not even enough, his biceps not firm enough, and his height insufficient to date a girl of Very's. But he seemed to care about her, seemed to value her ideas, seemed to need her laughter at his silly jokes. She had so little experience with longer than a two-week summer romance, she wasn't sure if what he had to offer was sufficient or the right thing to offer. But when he got her alone one night, and he gently began to explore her suppressed sexual longings, she knew what she wanted.

He smelled of clean soap, a dab of aftershave, an undercurrent of manly sweat. His hands were gentle, but insistent and sure. She found herself groaning with desire, and half expected a snarky laugh, instead, he matched her desire with his own. The kissing and petting that she had experienced with other 'boyfriends' left her with a feeling of consternation. A feeling that there should be, had to be, something more and better. Frankie gave her that more and better. Sex was fun, exciting, fulfilling and she wanted more. She understood what the cheap romantic novels were talking about.

She heard him talk about the band, listened to his guitar playing, badly executed, and his exciting stories of travels around the US. The weeks flew by, blending into one another. It was in the depths of a foggy night, parked in Frankie's car, that she admitted to him, and most of all to herself, that their childish antics had resulted in the consequence that every parent feared would, and every young couple knew couldn't, happen to them. She hadn't been to the doctor yet, but she knew the symptoms. After that, their lovemaking was routine, almost boring, and devoid of the heights of passion that she had experienced.

It was perfunctory, a part of the pact, the bargain they had made. They were now a couple and they did what couples do, married couples.

On the timetable, Very put in the date in tiny letters, then the fatal date of the movie. She skipped the date of the wedding, that she would never forget, and then, her part seemed done. She also skipped years ahead and put in the date of the finding the body in the orchard, the thing that had brought this all to light.

She went back to the photos. She stared at the photo of Danny Boy and Babe. She squinted and made their faces blurry, then brought them back into focus. Then the 'mist,' that out of focus feeling, the lightheadedness, the dizziness, began again. Where did this come from? How did it start? How will it end? What does it have to do with these two people? What part do they play in her story? Isn't this her story? Or is this story about Danny Boy and what happened to him?

Chapter Sixteen: First Day as a Private Investigator

The phone call that Very made the next morning was short, no nonsense, only a warning of attendance. Darrell said he awaited her appearance.

When Very was settled in her desk, had adjusted her chair to as high as it would go and stored her bag and belongings in an empty drawer, Darrell asked how it was going. Very, in a strict chronological order, reported her findings, referring to her notebook. She made a vague reference to her 'chart' timeline, wanting to keep that to herself for the time being. She felt it contained too much sexual energy for the time being. Later, when the memories faded from it, she could show it to Darrell. The photos from the yearbooks at the library were added to the overall stash. Darrell was excited that Very had found the names of the boys in the band, but was anxious to get Very started on finding Frankie.

"Being methodical is the key. You need to search with a system, checking every database to the end. If you were fairly certain that Frankie Monroe was out there, on social media, working etc., then it would be easy to find him right away. But the fact that he never contacted his mother, or his sister, that he seemed to just disappear, means that he did disappear. Or at least, wanted us to believe that he was no longer alive. Therefore, we have to do a thorough search as if he was trying to hide his existence. In other words, we need to find out that he is not out there, in the next town, using the same name. Does that make sense? First, we try to find the person by pretending that they are still using their real name and ID. And only when that doesn't work, we assume that the person has deliberately disappeared. People try it all the time. Usually when they want to avoid paying alimony or child support. Another thing is to fly the coop leaving a spouse behind, who then collects the life insurance. That is a really dumb thing to do, I don't know why people keep trying that one."

"Too much TV. They think that the TV writers are writing about real things." Very laughed. Her mother had liked to watch mysteries on TV, even the true crime ones, although she preferred the British cozies. "So, what happens when people try to disappear and the spouse tries to collect the insurance?"

"Aha, that's where someone like me comes in. Insurance companies hate cases without bodies. So, unless there is a corpse, companies will insist on the seven-year rule and let the court decide. Seven years is a long time to wait to collect insurance. That's why there are instances of big fires with too many claims and not enough corpses, or disasters with out of state missing persons. Someone will take the opportunity to hide a disappearance in a place where no body will ever be found. Mount St. Helens is an example. Who was up there when the volcano blew? Few people, but there were a lot of claims filed after that one. Hah, even fewer payouts."

"So, where do we start?" Very picked up her notebook.

"In the most obvious places and with the most obvious names. First, we start with the California databases, then go on to the neighboring states, widening the circle as we go. We start with Frank and then try the variations that are possible. Frank is short for Francis, so that is an easy one. You said you called him Frankie, so try that one as well. We could try just F. Monroe. Or Franklin, another variation of Frank. Or Francisco? And as I think Frank Monroe is going to be a very common name, we will have to go in with a date of birth or age. If someone is going to try and disappear, they may alter their birthdate, usually the year or month or make it a day earlier or later. People usually are smart enough to not place their age too far from their true age because that is a giveaway that they have something to hide. However much you want to not be 'old', shaving 20 years off your age is a bad idea."

"Because of looks, gray hair wrinkles and so forth, we can usually place someone, huh?" Very added.

"So where were you when Kennedy was shot?" Darrell turn to Very.

"I was in eighth grade, I remember the school principal coming into the classroom."

"So, if you said you were ten years younger, you would probably have had no memory of that day. Even five years younger and you would remember it differently. That's why it's a bad idea to change your ago too much."

"Where were you?" Very asked.

Darrell threw his head back and snorted with laughter. "I wasn't even born yet. Hard to compare notes on that one."

Darrell turned back to his computer. "These programs are also loaded or accessible on that computer. This is where they are; this is how you access them. Some of them I've had to pay for the access to. Some of them are free. Some are limited, meaning only five or ten searches per month. If I want more, I have to pay.

"Let's start here in California, free database." Darrell swiftly showed Very how to do it. He tried one variation of Frank and then another. He scrolled through and found a number of Frank Monroe's and then skipped all those outside the age range. "You have all this down so you can eliminate this database?"

"Wait, what's this one called?" Very busied herself with notes and hints, filling page after page.

Darrell noted which ones were 'accurate' and which ones just stole information from other databases. "That means that once you have searched the government sponsored or free ones, then the ones that simply repeat what you can easily find should be ignored." He turned back to the search.

"Oh," Darrell interrupted himself. "What about this one, really close match." He clicked on a link and a business profile sprang up. Photo, CV, testimonials.

Very turned and leaned over Darrell's shoulder. "But he's black," Very stated the obvious.

"Hmmm, take note. Because he seems really close to what we're looking for, he may come up again. And he is not your Frankie."

"Yeah. Okay, I think I'm ready to get started." She clicked and clicked and saw a list of one database by state. "You have to do each state separately here?" she whined.

Darrell swiveled his chair and spoke directly to her. "This is a treasure hunt, a needle in a haystack scenario, burrowing in the mud as in mudlark, in fact the very definition of a skip tracer. And this is just the US. He could have gone to Canada or Mexico. Do you know how many Americans live in Mexico? Do you comprehend how easy it is to nip over the border to Canada and make a new life? So, we start in California and work outwards. It gets easier as you go, don't worry."

Very turned her chair around, with her back to Darrell and got to it. She took a break and went to the ladies' room down the hall, using a key that Darrell had. When she returned, she asked in a timid voice. "Any chance of a cup of coffee?"

Darrell appeared elated as he jumped up and threw open a door in a high cabinet tucked into a corner of the minuscule office. Above were office supplies, and below, tucked into a tiny space, was a personal-sized fridge. On the shelf above sat an electric kettle, a French press coffee maker and various tea bags, coffee sacks, and an assortment of sugars, both real and fake.

"Oh," Very cooed admiringly. "Creamer?"

Darrell opened the fridge to reveal fake and real creamers, as well as cookies.

"Wow, all you need is a bed and you are set, your own hidey-hole."

Darrell's cheeks colored and he used his foot to point underneath his desk. Very bent down to peek and saw a rolled-up yoga mat and a small nylon bag that she was sure held a light-weight sleeping bag.

"Really?" Very laughed.

"Sometimes, just occasionally, I do stake outs and this is easier than running around to and from home or a hotel." He stopped on this lame note.

Very made some coffee, for both of them, in the French press. She put real cream into a small cup and savored the aroma and flavor. She and Darrell found they both liked their coffee the same way. Thick and dark, but with a dash of cream to lighten it up. Very took a little sugar in hers, Darrell more. They talked coffee for the time it took them to finish their cups and then went back to work.

They took a break and walked to Bill Lee's Bamboo Chopsticks for lunch. They both ordered a lunch special, which was a huge amount of food. They laughed that they did this as they planned on having leftovers. Darrell said, "I don't like to cook." Very admitted that since her mother died, she had come to rely on leftovers more and more. Properly cooking for one was difficult, so dozens of plastic containers were her personal frozen food section.

"I'll add at least half of this, if not more, to my stash. Mmmm, love the sweet and sour. Although the fried rice is a bit inauthentic, I still like it." Very said while digging in with the chopsticks she had asked for.

Darrell complimented her on her chopstick use, which Very laughed at. "I've been using chopsticks all my life. I taught myself using this." She held up the package the chopsticks came in, which had vivid diagrams on the side. One, two, three. "I think it's funny when someone, almost always Asian, compliments me, as if being white means your fingers can't learn how to manipulate these little bits of wood. Humph!"

"So, do you ever cook?" Very continued the conversation.

"Oh, I am not without some talent in that department, but I don't have that much interest in the mechanics of it. I do like to eat," he patted his belly. "And since I live alone, I am forced to do some food preparation. I've thought about a dog, some companionship, but…"

"Too much work? Have to walk them, you know. And they can get possessive and want too much attention, bored and bark too much, get sick and cost a lot of money. Says she who has a cat and worries about vet bills. I think you are better off without."

"My main recreation is bird watching and you can't take a dog with you, the dog barks and scares the birds away. And I often go with friends and they would hate it, I'd be blackballed. And then when I go on vacations, or away for weekends, what would I do with a dog?"

They continued in this vein, sharing stories of their lives, Darrell telling Very about his two brothers, one in Texas, another in Washington. He rambled on about how he came to Bakersfield for college and never left. His parents were gone now and he didn't have any plans for the future, just moseying on down the road of life.

Back at the office, Very got started in again on more databases. She admitted that it was becoming easier as she negotiated the wealth of names, variations and myriad ways to be 'Frank Monroe'. Only one in a hundred caused her pause. And she began to realize that trying to find her Frank Monroe was an outside chance. If he was hiding, he must have taken another name.

Suddenly the phone rang. Darrell picked up the receiver of an old, old black rotary phone that had been hidden under a pile of paper. "Yes, yes, yes. Okay, I'm on my way now."

Darrell looked up at Very, whose eyes bugged out at the antique phone. "Oh, it's a fake, it has a digital component underneath. Gift from a friend who thought it went with the gold lettering on the door. I have to go now.

Here's a key, lock up when you leave. See you tomorrow?"

"Yeah, bye." Suddenly, Very felt lonely. She had been working all day, but the companion at her back, along with the coffee and lunch had made the experience enjoyable. She wrapped up the database, made a few notes and left as well.

At home, she slipped the Chinese food into the fridge. She got a Diet Coke out of the pantry, put ice into a glass and went outside to the patio. The cat wandered by and Very unconsciously let her hand drift down to pet her furry companion.

Clouds in the sky gathered quickly and Very absently watched their shapes growing, morphing, swirling, and changing colors: white, gray, black, dirty brown. Sunlight flitted around the outsides of the strange shapes and the edges sharpened and then blurred in a growing tumult. The first boom of thunder was in the distance, but soon the sounds moved nearer. Very sat and drank her Coke, watching the storm come closer. It was early for rain, being only September, and she dismissed the creeping coolness as a fake harbinger of winter. The storm oozed closer, filling the sky with heaving, moving moisture. The flash of lightening was unexpected and the cat dashed under the table, crouching behind Very, anticipating the noise to follow.

The thunder rolled, visceral in its volume and power. It faded after a few seconds and Very watched as the clouds took on a greenish tinge. The light, a jagged vein of power, lit the sky only nanoseconds before the crash broke over the scene. Very screamed involuntarily and stood, knocking her drink to the cement slab on the patio where the shatter of the glass was muted by the aftermath of the lightning strike. The smell of burning chemicals filled her nostrils and she began to shake with fear. If she had been just a few feet further outside, it might have struck her.

Well, a lightning strike had appeared in her life, changing everything she had known about herself, her past and what might have been the fabric of her life. It was the finding of the body in the orchard that had started it all, but the aftermath was still unknown.

Chapter Seventeen: Q-Ball and Curly

Very called Darrell first thing on Saturday morning. "Sorry about this, but can I go into the office today? I need to start searching for these characters, you know, the boys in the band."

"Sure, I need to go in as well, left over business from yesterday. See you about 9:30?"

They met at the front door, precisely at 9:30. Very looked at her wristwatch and back at Darrell. "Hmmmm, on time, precisely on time. A little OCD?"

"I could say the same about you!"

"Takes one to know one." They laughed together as they entered the office.

Very related what she had found on a preliminary search the night before on her own computer. "I found some addresses, though none seem to be current. But they do seem to have lived in Bakersfield at some time in the past. Perhaps even recently. I don't think they are living in these addresses now, but I don't know where to find them, if anywhere. Maybe they're homeless."

"I'll show you how to use the reverse address directories. They are on your computer there. Bakersfield is easy, it's not a big city. I'll also show you how to search the newspaper files, and some of the police arrest files. I'll bet the two of them will show up on those. We have lots of places to look for them, including registered sex offenders, DMV records and all. When you know where you want to look next, just ask me. I'm here."

Very opened her notebook and started a page for Q-Ball, Stanley Leon. She wrote down what information she had on him, probable DOB and an address she had found the night before, transferring that information from a random page in the back. She silently chided herself for being sloppy in her notekeeping.

She found some information from the DMV. Six foot one, 150 pounds. Tall and skinny, as he looked in the yearbook and the photo from Babe Harger. But further searches gave a dead end. "You said that you can access prison or arrest records?"

"You ready for that? It's not pretty. You might have to read a lot about unsavory things."

"I got myself into this. I guess I need to face the unprincipled evil that lurks in the corners and recesses of my life. It seems strange that these are people that had strings of connections to my own life. I just have never, or very seldom, had to deal with the underbelly. Even the kids at school, who I knew had relatives 'inside', their problems or concerns rarely impacted me. Their lives didn't abut mine in that way. But now, I might be looking for people with criminal behavior problems, who have documents verifying their evil wrong-doing. Am I really doing this?"

"Welcome to my world. Tell me when you find out anything of value, that might connect to Frankie." Darrell turned back to his own work.

Very cruised around the websites, building up a picture of Q-Ball. He had been arrested, and convicted, of dealing drugs. The newspaper had coverage of his trial. Very read and shivered with distaste at the details oozing from the pages of the newspaper coverage. The facts were bare, but dripped with implications of moral turpitude. Drugs sold to minors, at venues that attracted high school students. She looked closely at the grainy black and white photo that accompanied the notice of sentencing. What little hair he had, had been whacked off by prison officials, or shaved. The round, regular shape of his head, smooth and ready to roll across the billiard table, highlighted the photos. Not once, however, did the paper use his nickname, which seemed so obvious. Indeed, it must have seemed obvious to everyone that this man's head resembled a billiard ball.

A few years on and another trial photo showed a more mature, weighing an extra ten pounds, but equally bald, Stanley Leon. This time the sentence was longer.

But in between, there was a notice of a band with one Stanley (Cue Ball) Leon. Coupled with Stanley's name was that of Curly Wilson.

A notice of a hearing of a request for early release, for good behavior, was accompanied by yet another photo, this one showing an equally bald, but more presentable Stanley. There was no notice of the success, or lack thereof, of the hearing, but there was one more mention of Stanley Leon.

The band was named as 'The Band of Two Men'. Two men stood side by side, guitars slung over their shoulders, leaning in towards each other. It was a staged photo, like a professional photographer would have orchestrated to create an image of harmony, fellowship and compatibility of minds and hearts to an adoring public. The name, 'The Band of Two Men', oh so original.

"What have you found?" Darrell asked, turning in his chair.

"Another band picture. Look," she moved aside to let Darrell see.

"Great, make sure you copy it. Actually, you can just copy all of it. Or maybe not. Keep notes, though, so you can go back. Photos, keep those; articles, make notes. Those are my recommendations."

Very continued searching for another half hour, and found nothing more on Q-Ball. It was as if he, too, had disappeared. The band had disappeared, and even the legal issues faded from the pages of the local rag. It was a disappointment, but she moved on to Curly.

Very had found a senior photo in the newspaper. He had graduated a year later than Danny, something that Very hadn't expected. But he had been awarded a music scholarship and so had earned a place in a long list of award winners. The cap that sat on top of his immense pile of hair sat in a precarious position, like a crown balanced on a pouf of cotton candy. The black and white photo rendered the hair an off-white color. Cotton candy perhaps?

She also found a short piece on an arrest for drugs, similar to Q-Ball's. If anyone had noticed, it seemed incongruous that one year after he had graduated with a scholarship, Curly, aka Glenn Wilson, had now found himself on the wrong side of the law. Very also found the same story with the two young men with guitars. And then she found another, longer article.

"Young man with a voice like Johnny Cash will go far." A country-western reviewer from out of town had gone to a performance of 'The Band of Two Men' and written a gushing review, concentrating on Curly's voice. "The deep bass and croak of a classic Johnny Cash voice makes this performer stand out." There was no photo attached. She read the review twice and then decided to save it. There was an undercurrent of praise for Curly and disdain for the talents of Q-Ball which seemed uncomfortably unfair.

Another interview, only eight months later, also concentrated on Curly. In it, the same journalist quoted extensively from a rambling series of encounters with Curly. "Yeah," Curly was quoted, "I've played with a whole series of guys in the last eight years. The latest one is Q-Ball Leon. They call him that because he's got no hair, never had any. Born that way, die that way." Similar ramblings followed, but she began to see a picture of Curly, his relationships with his band mates and others. He was on his second marriage at this time, even though he was still in his twenties.

Darrell interrupted, "Are you hungry? We could go out and get something?"

Very looked up from the computer screen at Darrell, then down at her watch. "Gosh, I should be hungry. I've been at this for hours, but…"

Darrell looked distraught. Clearly, he wanted to share a meal with Very, but his professionalism edged out his desires. He peeked at the screen in front of her. "Found something?"

"Yeah, and it seems really relevant, or at least it's interesting and I just want to keep going now." Torn, between hunger and fascination with the search.

"Bloodhound on the scent. I know the feeling. I think you will make a great detective one day. Most people find this really tedious and boring, but you seem to have latched onto it well."

Very looked startled and responded with a wide grin. "Thank you for the compliment, that was very generous of you."

Darrell blushed an unbecoming shade of purple and mumbled something incomprehensible.

"I'm sorry, I didn't mean to embarrass you. It's just that modern society seems so cruel and full of put-downs that some of us teachers learned to counter that negativity by handing out extra positivity where we encounter it. Sorry, I sounded like a high-school teacher." Very waited briefly for a reaction, then went on. "Look, buy me a sandwich and we can eat it together here when you get back. Fair enough? And then I can read this article to my heart's content."

Darrell nodded with a frisson of uncertainty and left quickly.

Very returned to the article. She took notes of anything that seemed factually important. Like the two wives, no names though. There was a bizarre mention of an arson attempt. Someone was apparently looking for him, but went to the wrong home, and started a fire that caused damage and injuries. "The guy said he was looking for me, Glenn Wilson, but got the address for this poor jerk, Glen Wilshire, and then burned him out. Why someone would do that, I don't know. Never heard of the guy anyway." No name was given for the erstwhile arsonist. Very made a note of the time of the arson attack and planned to look it up later. The article ended with a note that more reporting from the interview would come in a subsequent issue of the paper.

The door banged open and Darrell burst in. "I forgot to ask what you wanted, so I got vegetarian, is that okay? Please say it's okay! You got vegetarian the last time, so I figured you were that kind of person, although you did get meat when we ate Chinese, but lots of ladies these days don't eat meat, or much of it, I have heard, so I got vegetarian. It looks really good, there's avocado and sprouts, and oh, I got the sauce separately, I didn't know if you wanted all that stuff dripping all over you and getting on your clothes and…"

"It's fine, vegetarian is fine. You did very well." Very sidestepped the elaborate compliment of last time, but attempted to stop the stream of consciousness flow of explanations. She bit her tongue before 'good job' came out.

They ate in the silence of hunger for a few minutes before Darrell interrupted with, "What have you found so far?"

"Curly had a Johnny Cash-like voice and was going far in the Bakersfield music scene. Q-Ball was a side-kick or partner. Some details about drug arrests and oh, Curly was on wife number two before he was thirty. But no real clues. I have more to look for." Very wrapped up the other half of her sandwich and turned back to the screen.

She searched the next couple of days of the paper, but no follow-up article was to be found. She looked at the next week, but again, no luck. She went back to the original article and checked the author. She searched again, finally finding the rest of the interview and more, a month later.

The headline ran, "Johnny Cash (the reincarnation) headlines at Trout's." The rest of the interview was interspersed with the adoring, gushing, lavish praise for the latest Cash wannabe who was currently appearing at Trout's every Friday night. The reporter noted that Curly had just had a new suit made in LA by one of the top makers of Western wear for performers and would be debuting his new duds that coming weekend. The article

oozed onto the next page and Very found herself
wondering why she had bothered looking up this one.
Filling in the column inches were three short paragraphs
that appeared as though they had been cut from the
original interview, weeks before. Very had heard about
this quaint practice from the journalism teachers. Editors
had to fill column inches. Stories were just as often as not
required to have a particular number of words in order to
fill a particular space. If an article was too long, the editor
could happily just leave an article dangling in mid
paragraph. Or the article could have some nonsense added
at the end that was only vaguely connected to the topic,
just to make it fit the physical space.

This short section had obviously been cut from the
previous article and attached here as a filler. The storyline
did not flow properly. Very read, then stopped at the
truncated third paragraph. "Yeah, I've played with a lot of
guys over the years. Of course, my good friend and back
up guitarist, Q-Ball Leon, often had others join us, a
variety of buddies, over the years. Of course, we were
always the core, but you had Dan, Frank, Jose, and lots of
guys, including Killer. They all played with us at one time
or another."

Very read the names again. There was Danny Boy
Harger. Jose or Joe. And Killer? Who was he? But there
was also Frank. This was it. This was the first time that
she had a connection between Q-Ball, Curly, Danny Boy
and Frankie Monroe. But was this 'Frank' who played
with Curly, her Frank?

She needed to ask Babe Harger a few more questions.
And this time, she would listen to no more lies.

Chapter Eighteen: Return to the Harger Home

On Sunday morning, Very waited until 'after church' to call Babe Harger. She listened to Babe's less than forceful voice, but did not take 'no' for an answer. She raided the fridge and pantry for some goodies to take, but in the end, stopped at the store for some nice cheese, fancy crackers and a plate of fruit, already cut into slices and cubes. She nabbed a box of chocolate covered cookies as she headed to the checkout counter. Years of caring for her mother had taught her what old ladies liked, and were capable of eating easily. She would have taken ice cream, but feared it would melt, so promised herself another time. Her mother had adored ice cream and it was the last solid food she had eaten. Older people liked it, she wasn't quite sure why.

The drive up the hill to Tehachapi was no less nerve-wracking, even though it was Sunday. The semi-trucks careened around the curves and she cautiously let them get in front of her, even though it meant driving slower than she wanted. Better slower than squeezed up against the traffic divider by a mechanical behemoth. The trees here had started to change colors, and a hillside of orange and red could be seen in the distance. This time, she drove straight to the modest home. More cars were parked on the street than before, but it was Sunday afternoon, visiting grandma day, or sleeping on the couch day, or at least not a working day.

As Very got out of her car, she noticed clouds forming over the mountains. It was a little early for rain, but it was the right time of year for unsettled weather. As she watched, one cloud with a dark gray underbelly began to grow a pompadour of frothy ice cream foam, reaching for the clear blue sky. Very walked across the street, carrying her tray and plastic bags of offerings.

She knocked on the door, then rang the doorbell. Hearing no sound from within of the bell, she knocked again, this time louder. She hesitated, listening for the 'slap-slap' of slippers approaching. Nothing. She knocked again. She reached out and tried the doorknob. It slipped easily in her hand, the door smoothly opening inward on silent hinges.

"Babe," Very called quietly. The living room was empty, but with that lived-in look that let a visitor know that the occupant had just left. "Babe, are you here?"

A figure appeared at what must have been the bedroom doorway. "You here?" she said.

"Yes, Babe, I've brought you some things to eat. Would you like me to make you a plate?"

"Naw, just take 'em to the kitchen," she answered, shuffling into the living room, heading for her seat on the couch. Very watched over her shoulder as she deposited things in the kitchen. She noticed that Babe trailed a small cylinder on wheels after herself. A tube ran up to her head where a headpiece encircled her unruly mop of hair before dipping down to sit below her nose, poking little plastic straws into her nostrils.

Very grabbed a plate, tore into the package of crackers and threw some on the plate along with a slice of cheese. She reentered the living room in time to help Babe seat herself. "Here's something. Would you like something to drink?"

"Yes, fizzy lime, lemon, whatever." Babe deflated into the cushions, moving to find her comfort spot.

Very returned with a glass of fizzy drink that she had found in the fridge, along with a couple of ice cubes. She placed it on the scarred coffee table, this time without hesitation. "Are you feeling well today?"

"What do you think?" Babe snarled at Very.

"I think you were better the other day. Today is not one of those good days, I guess." She had trouble thinking of Babe as of her own generation as she acted more like her mother. One foot in the grave, her father would have said.

Very talked slowly, trying to politely wiggle into Babe's good graces, now that she had turned up out of the blue, and on a bad day, too. "I came here today to see if you had any more information about your husband and his band. You know, Curly and Q-Ball? You let me see the picture of them. Well, I've found out some more. They weren't very nice characters, were they?"

"Rotten, both of them, born rotten. I didn't like Danny running with them. But they had a band, the three of them, they were buddies from high school. They tried to get Danny to come sing and play with them again. I fought him on that. He was going to be a father, he had to go get a real job. And he needed to stay home with me in the evenings. He didn't need to go out all day and night."

"Did you know anything about drugs? You know, Q-Ball and Curly both got caught with drugs?"

"Drugs? I don't know anything about drugs. God forbid that Danny would get involved with drugs. I mean, smoking a little weed now and then isn't drugs, is it? But dealing, were they dealing?"

"I think so. Was Danny involved with them when they did drugs?" She asked this softly, trying to downplay the latent accusation in the question.

"Drugs, bad things? Danny? I don't know, I never knew anything about that. Just the running around, the maryjane. Well, maybe the others, but I told Danny that he couldn't do that, he was a married man, he needed to act like one. But he said that he could make money. You know, they all worked in the oil fields. It was hard work, they got dirty, they got hurt, they got laid off, or fired. Those bosses were mean. Sometimes they'd be forced to quit, then they couldn't get unemployment. No reason, just so the company wouldn't have to pay so much unemployment. Mean bastards, those guys. But oil field jobs were not that easy to get, you needed to know somebody. And you had to keep your nose clean and be super nice to the boss. But those two, Curly and Q-Ball, they thought they were too good to get their hands dirty in the fields. So, they used to go to LA and buy the stuff, I don't know what kind of stuff, I didn't want to know. And they would sell it and they wanted my Danny to help them. I wouldn't let him. I told him to stay away from those two crooks. But you know, it's so hard to do that. It's so hard to make some silly little boy, who thinks he's a man, believe that it was really, really stupid to get involved with those two. Bastards! It was their fault, they trapped him." Babe leaned back into the couch after this harangue.

"Let me get you some fruit, there's melon," Very said, getting up, letting Babe sink into her thoughts.

Very sat quietly with Babe as she ate a little cheese and a cracker. When she tried a wedge of watermelon, she began to choke.

Very expertly took it away from her and put a napkin to Babe's face, urging her to spit it out. Gently, she folded the rejected food into the paper and put it aside. She waited for Babe to stop coughing and helped her drink a bit. Very hoped she had help at other times. It could be dangerous for old people, choking on food they tried to feed themselves.

"So, can you tell me if there were other friends? Like 'Joe' or 'Jose'?" Very tried again.

"Smith, there was a Smith. But Joe? Not Jose, no one with that name, unless maybe he called himself Joe. But maybe it was Joe Smith. What a name, huh? Who wants a name that half the country has? But I don't remember that one."

Very let her rest a bit more. She wanted to introduce Frankie's name again, but the last time she heard that name, she was quite sure she didn't know him. What was the other weird name? Killer?

"Was another one, 'Killer'?"

"Who was a killer? They were all friends, well maybe they were friends, at least they said they were." Babe sighed and shut her mouth tightly, holding it closed with a rictus.

Very let her sit and think a minute. Babe had been clear, then acted confused. She recognized the signs of dementia, but wondered how far gone she was. Some information sounded logical, other bits sounded like rants from the past. She seemed to know that Danny was probably dealing drugs with his friends, his bandmates and workmates? It appeared as though she did, but wanted to forget it. And what was their fault?

"Where's Cassandra? She said she was coming. She doesn't have to knock, I told her that. She can just come in, it's okay." Babe leaned forward, now being anxious.

Very then understood why the door had been unlocked. Babe was waiting for her daughter.

"Cassandra is your daughter?"

"Cassandra, the big beautiful name. She didn't like it, she didn't want a big name, she wanted a normal name. Wanted to be 'Sandy', or maybe 'Cassie', not Cassandra. Why did I bother to give her a really beautiful, great name? And then she doesn't want it!" Babe nursed her grievance by reaching for another sip of fizzy lime.

"My mother did the same to me. I forgive you and I forgive her. We didn't change our names, did we, Cassandra and I? We just made them easier for the rest of the world, for us and for our friends." She had never let her mother forget that she had been saddled with an impossible name, but maybe her mother felt as Babe did. Give your child a big beautiful name, not something ordinary. But it was no guarantee of gratitude, the giving of a name. It could so easily backfire. You could have a Mary who desperately wants to be Madeline, a Bob who wants to be Rupert, or an Ann who would rather be Annabelle, or the other way around. But it was impossible to know when you chose a name for an unborn child.

"Where is Cassandra? She always comes on Sunday and she makes my lunch. She should be here."

"Does she live nearby? Maybe there's traffic or something." Very tried to sound out Babe.

"No idea where she lives these days. Stays here, stays there. What kind of life is that for a grown woman? I blame it all on that piece of shit she married. The second time around is always better, she said. Hah! Why did wife number one and two give him the heave-ho? Better stay away from those men. And it isn't as if she needed any more kids. Two wild boys. And where do they live? God only knows. I don't see them often enough to even ask which parent or friend or county appointed guardian has them these days. They're practically grown in any case. Ready to be on their own. But the new husband has his own family, so he's not interested in being a father. Pah. All of them. Only Cassandra is good to me. She's all I've got, all I've ever had. Well, I had my folks and my brothers, truly they helped a lot. But they're all gone, or scattered. So, it's just Cassandra and me. But, where is she? She should be here. What time is it?" Babe twisted in her seat to have a look at a clock that sat on the buffet where the photos were kept.

A knock came on the door and a woman burst into the room. She carried two large grocery bags and a harried look. "Mom? You okay? Sorry I'm late."

Very stood and faced the newcomer. "Cassandra Harger?"

Cassandra stepped back a bit when faced with this newcomer. "Yeah. And you are?"

"Very Blew. I came here the other day to visit your mother. I'm looking for information. I just came again, in case she remembered anything else."

"Yeah, I think she said that someone was here, asking about Dad. Yeah, really sad. Or maybe not."

Very stared at Cassandra and said nothing more. She took in the eyes, big, round and with a hint of gold striped in the brown. Her hair was dark brown, curly, and it formed a straight line across her wide forehead. She had a snub nose and a wide, generous mouth. Her body was compact, with strong broad shoulders and she held herself with a barely concealed intensity, as if someone was behind her, about to chase her. She was poised to win.

Very now understood what it was that Babe Harger was lying about.

It would not take a blood test, or a DNA test, to tell her who Cassandra was. She was unmistakably Frankie Monroe's daughter.

Chapter Nineteen: Frankie's Daughter

Very looked at Cassandra, trying not to stare. She did not know what to say. She was a stranger in Babe's home, feeding her, and one who was obviously not well. She needed to close down her face, which she knew, from experience, could be read by any fifteen-year-old who had misbehaved. Did she look as if she was hiding something? Say nothing. Think before you speak. Smile, be innocuous.

"Mom? Mom? You okay?" Cassandra approached Babe and looked at her. Unable to extricate herself from the bags, she leaned closer and shouted. "What are you eating?"

Babe looked up, a blank, confused face answered Cassandra's question. She wasn't aware of what she had been eating, or even if she had been eating. She knew that look, one that had plagued her mother in the last few months of her life. Very backed away and let daughter and mother communicate, in whatever way they did.

"Maybe I can come back later. I didn't mean to interfere. When I was here before, she was fine. I had no idea. It's just cheese and crackers and some fruit." Very mumbled apologetically.

She watched Cassandra take the plate away and then try to pick up the bags of groceries.

"Let me help you," Very offered, grabbing the bigger of the two bags and heading for the kitchen.

"Thanks, I didn't mean to imply that what she was eating was bad, but she's on a diet. What is she drinking? Cassandra spied the fizzy lemon bottle sitting on the counter. "Oh, no, not that stuff again. Mom, where did you get this lemonade from? You know it has too much sugar. She has diabetes and we are trying to watch the sugar intake. Oh, could you do something for me? Get her glass and put lots of ice cubes in it. That way it will melt and she will get some water with her sugar fix. At least these other things are not bad, they're okay. But I need to watch everything. She is not used to denying herself anything. The diagnosis is new, so we are both trying to figure it out."

"Sorry, I had no idea. Is she really bad today? I found her rather coherent before, so I was a bit surprised to see the oxygen and now to hear this. I'm sorry. What can I do? I'll help put away these groceries, you can look after her." Very started taking items out of bags., But she wasn't going to put much away. Putting things in cupboards in a stranger's house was the last thing she wanted to do today.

Very listened as Cassandra asked her mother how she was, if she was hungry and if she needed anything. Very made a quick trip into the living room where she snatched the offending fizzy lemonade, filled up the glass with ice cubes and snuck it back to the place near Babe's hand where she had taken it from.

Very put as many things away as she dared, uncertain if she should gather up the offending offerings she had brought, but decided to wait on Cassandra's final verdict of suitability. She finally wandered back into the living room, where Cassandra was adjusting Babe's oxygen.

"Thanks for bringing the food, I'm sorry I was so quick to take it away. I usually make dinner later in the afternoon. The doctor says it's important for diabetics to eat regularly, not haphazardly. Like snacking, and drinking forbidden sugary drinks. That wasn't your fault. I found out that one of my sons brought it over a few days ago. She loves it. But she had him hide it too. She knows she's not allowed."

"Yeah, I understand. I lived with my mother until she died last year. She was always so with it, so coherent, that it was sad in the end to see her lose her way. I found it difficult to deny her the favorite foods she had come to like. So, I get it." Very sat down on the love seat, at the end of the couch.

She wanted to stay. She needed to get more information and did not want to lose the opportunity. The list of questions that she had for both mother and daughter began to grow exponentially in her mind. Could she surreptitiously get out her notebook and make some notes? She rejected that idea. She just needed to remember everything she was told.

"So, Cassandra, do you live nearby? I asked Babe and she didn't know where you were living."

"Oh, no wonder she doesn't know, I barely know. Well, I moved out a couple of weeks ago, or rather, I tried to get my soon-to-be-ex to move out. But he wasn't budging. I thought I could just live alongside him, you know, not speak to him and so forth. But that didn't work. The only thing we wanted to do was yell at each other. It would have been better if we hadn't been in the same space, but he refused to leave. Well, he will move out when I get my house back. After that fiasco, I moved in with a girlfriend, but her boyfriend made a pass at me, so that was a no-go. Then I moved to another girlfriend's extra room, but her husband is due back next week from his job and I already know that one. Spaghetti hands. So, I really don't know where I'm living."

Very looked around, trying to figure out if there was an extra room in this house or why an obvious solution to the problem of Mom and a place to live hadn't occurred to Cassandra.

"I guess the easiest thing is to move in here. Not the best arrangement, but…" Cassandra mused. "I'm thinking she might need to go to a home soon. I have a job and when I work, that's a lot of hours to be away."

"You could get some home help. I know it's not cheap, but it would mean you could still work and look after your mom. That's what I did in the end. It meant she stayed at home until the very end." She tried to relax into the 'helpful confidante' narrative, all the while keeping a close eye on Cassandra.

Very studied her face. What were the details she could remember from years ago of Frankie's face? The nose, the hairline, the color and texture of her hair was amazingly similar. Cassandra was about two or three inches shorter than her own 5'9", which she knew was Frankie's height as well. So, his daughter was of average height. Very tried to estimate her weight, slightly heavy, but a solid, compact build, which was Frankie's bulk. She could put her arms around him, but he filled them with muscles and his frame. She tried not to stare. Then, Cassandra put her right hand on her chin and rubbed it, three times, before letting her hand drift down her neck, placing it on her voice box for a short beat, before dropping it. Very tried very, very hard not to show any emotion at the gesture. It was a signature Frankie move. She never understood where it came from, what it meant, but it was a nervous gesture that was unique to him. And here she was, the woman Very KNEW was his daughter, using the same gesture. She could never have seen her father do this, could she? Or was that another one of Babe's lies? Did Cassandra know? How much was there to tell?

"Did your Mom tell you why I came?" Very asked cautiously once they were seated and comfortable.

"She did mention something, about Dad. Being found in the orchard and all. Apparently, he was murdered." Cassandra shivered. "That is awful, but I don't know what it has to do with us. I mean, he disappeared just a month before I was born, so I never saw him. He was only a photograph, and a threat when I misbehaved. I hope they can clear this up soon; I just feel so removed from it all. I mean, it's terrible that he was murdered, but what can anyone do at this point? Are they going to arrest my mother for killing my father and burying him in an orchard? She was nine months pregnant, and besides, why would she murder him? There was no money or anything. I mean, he not being here was a hole in my life, but... I guess Mom was a bit pissed at him for running away. And now, to think he didn't come back because he couldn't, he was dead. I don't think she's taken it in yet. And yeah, to get back to your question, she couldn't quite figure out what you wanted to know. Something about Dad's friends. And she let you see some photos."

"From the cigar box. Is that where Danny's photos are?"

"Oh, lots of photos. Years ago, I went through that box and took out some of my photos, the best ones, which I have. But a bunch of them were just cheap black and whites of a bunch of young guys. I didn't really care. I recognized a few of them as being of my dad, but that was all. Didn't care. Do I care now?"

They both looked at Babe, sitting quietly in her place on the couch, listening to the conversation.

"Mom, are you hungry? Ms. Blew is here, she can eat with us, is that okay? I'm hungry, let's go get something to eat. How about easy stuff today, soup and sandwiches? I'll do something better for tomorrow. Maybe I'll do a casserole, and leave it for you. Would you like that? But now, let's have a little something? Okay?"

The sing-song baby voice that Cassandra had adopted was cringeworthy, but then she recognized it as an 'old people' and 'young kids' voice. Cajoling five-year-olds was similar to wheedling eighty-five-year-olds or others who had declined in health. Very volunteered to help Cassandra in the kitchen and soon the three were seated at the small kitchen table eating sandwiches.

Babe rambled on about kittens and the flowers in the yard and the next-door neighbors, ignoring Very as much as possible. She grabbed at the plate of fruit, picking up each piece in her hands and rejecting any that she found unsatisfactory. Cassandra looked at her mother with disapproval, but did not stop her. Instead she rolled her eyes at Very in a 'what can a daughter/mother do' gesture. At one point, Babe got food caught in her oxygen tube and Cassandra helped her take it off. "We can do without this for a little while, can't we?" Cassandra cooed.

Very waited for an opportunity to get Cassandra alone again, planning on what she would say. Very wanted to look at the box again. She wanted to rifle through the photos, not just meekly peek at what Babe was willing to share with her. What could she say to Cassandra to get her to relinquish the cardboard treasure coffer?

Finally, Cassandra had had enough of food play and coaxed her mother into taking a nap, or at least having a rest. "I'll clean up here," Very offered.

Babe and her daughter disappeared into the other side of the house, while Very snatched plates and bowls off the table, rinsing them and planning on leaving them in the sink. That was when she realized there was no dishwasher. She gritted her teeth and quickly washed and put them in the dish drain on the countertop. She briskly dried her hands and headed for the living room.

She entered the room just as Cassandra returned from settling her mother. She looked towards the buffet cabinet and saw the object of her desire sitting out on top, right where Babe had left it a few days before. Saliva practically oozed from her mouth, as Very hungered at the thought of getting her hands on the box.

"Is she all settled in for an afternoon nap? My mother loved her naps." Very sat down as if she belonged.

"Did you know my dad?" Cassandra asked.

Very missed a beat, until she realized that Cassandra was speaking of Danny Boy Harger.

"No, I never met him, that I know of. I do think that he might have known my fiancé, so that's why I wanted to talk with your mother. And look at the box of photos."

"Well, I can ask her about that. See if she thinks it's okay to look, I don't see why not, but she has always been protective of this box. It has some really old family photos as well." Cassandra looked at the box sitting on the sideboard. "Who was your fiancé?"

"Frankie Monroe." Very said it slowly, watching Cassandra's face for any reaction or recognition. "He disappeared around the same time as your dad. And when I saw the notice in the paper, about the body in the orchard, well, I thought it was my Frankie. Turned out to be your dad. But it was all so coincidental. And so, I looked up your mom, hoping she might be able to tell me something." Very began to pluck nervously at her fingers. She wanted to blurt out what she knew, but knew the time wasn't propitious. She needed to wait.

Cassandra got up and retrieved the box from the sideboard. She sat down with it in her lap and continued talking. "Mom isn't so old, but she's always been a smoker, and I think, she's been diabetic longer than we all thought. She's aged so much in the last couple of years. I don't know what she remembers and what she doesn't. I think she has forgotten things and then, she remembers them."

"Well, I've got to get going don't want to take up any more of your time." Very said this in one long string as she had heard her mother do. The niceties, a prelude to escape, poured out easily. "Maybe I can come back and look at the photos again?"

"Yeah, sure, I'll go through them and let you look at the old ones, the ones that might tell you something. I just want to check with her first." Cassandra said this as she opened the box and began to sift through the thin squares of paper.

A noise from the bedroom caught Cassandra's attention, distracting her from the box. "Mom, is that you? Trying to sneak a ciggie? You know you can't smoke anymore. That oxygen! She is an accident just waiting to happen," Cassandra said turning to Very. "I've told her a million times. Sometimes I think she lights up when I'm not here. She's good at hiding the ashtray."

Very took one more greedy look at the box and stood. "I'll go now."

"Hey, I'll walk you out," Cassandra said as she hung onto the box, following Very to the front door.

They walked out to the front lawn and Very noted that the shadows had lengthened and the air had cooled. She had spent the whole afternoon.

"Thanks for coming and for the food. She likes the fruit, could you tell?"

Very turned back and looked at Frankie Monroe's daughter, standing with legs apart, just as her father used to do.

A strange popping noise came from the room to the right, the front bedroom. They both looked.

A louder pop broke the glass, which blew outwards and landed with a hundred tinkling sounds.

"Mom," screamed Cassandra, turning to the house and beginning to run.

Cassandra dropped the box, and as the lid flew back, old photos spilled onto the grass. Then a louder explosion burst through the air, throwing shock waves against the objects in the way of the blast. Cassandra screamed again and pushed harder towards the door.

Very bent to pick up the box and scooped the spilled photos into her large spacious bag. She headed towards the door as yet another boom, a smaller one, ruptured the silence of the Sunday afternoon.

Chapter Twenty: The Cigar Box

As the sirens receded, Very stood in the front yard, watching them go. Cassandra had gone with her mother, tears streaming down her face, mumbling about the foolishness of what happened.

"Don't worry," Very had said. "I'll lock up for you. I'm sure everything will be safe; the neighbors are watching. The guy across the street has brought over a big piece of plywood to cover the window. Everything here is okay, at least. You just take care of your mom."

"You can leave the key under the thing by the back door. You'll know which one," Cassandra had said as she stepped into the ambulance.

Very looked over her shoulder to see if other neighbors were watching as she reentered the house. She started with the kitchen, which had been left clean after lunch. She tidied a few things in the living room, then entered the bedroom. There was nothing she could do with the mess. The electricity had been cut to this side of the house, so no accidents could happen. Most of the furniture was a complete loss and the stench of burned plastic and cloth clouded the air. The plyboard patch was being nailed over the gaping hole in the side of the house which kept out the light, so Very was unable to see much, only that there had been extensive damage. It was a wonder Babe was still alive.

Very glanced around, trying to see if there was anything valuable that needed to be hidden or taken away. She rifled through an underwear drawer, and found a small stash of $20 bills. Why do we always put things like this into underwear drawers? Thieves always know where to look. She took the money and went to the living room, searched in the top drawer of the sideboard, found an unused 'return reply' envelope and put the money in it. She shoved this into her bag as well. Very glanced at the cigar box; its bulk filling the oversized purse. She tried to rearrange things to make it fit better, but a corner still stuck out.

Very walked through the house, turning off all the lights and appliances, except the fridge, locked the front door from the inside and slipped out the back door. She glanced down at the plain cement stoop and the flowerbeds beside it. Painted rocks, garden gnomes, and cheap plastic garden art littered the patch of rocky bed under a rose bush. Before she locked the door, Very looked at the collection and wondered which was the 'fake' with the key hole underneath. She reached for the bright green frog and turned it over. How did Cassandra know that she would 'know' which was the right one? She locked the door and hid the key, putting the ugly frog back into its depression next to the door.

Before she left the back door, she scrolled through her phone. Very had asked Cassandra for her number and she had rattled it off easily. Very hoped that she had got it right. She texted. "How's Mom. House secured."

She walked around the side of the house and into the front yard. She stood on the front step and surveyed the neighborhood. Many people had come out to watch and gawk when the explosion shattered the calm of their Sunday afternoon, but only the old man had offered to help. He hadn't offered, exactly, he had just arrived with the plywood and started nailing it up. Perhaps his wife had sent him. No one else approached to talk to Cassandra or Very, only a few stood near their doors or just behind their curtains, twitching the drapes. What was the cause of their unconcern, or standoffishness? She felt sure that her neighbors on the street where she had lived for years would be offering to help or at least come out of their houses to gather information and offer sympathy. Was it because Babe was the 'crazy lady' on the block? Had she offended her neighbors and therefore earned their disdain? Or was this a neighborhood where no one knew anyone else, and didn't care to? Like so many other places in modern life, perhaps this was a place where neighbors were only the people who lived next door, not the 'villagers' of past times. Very surveyed the quiet, empty street.

Her phone binged, Cassandra had texted back. "At Memorial in Bako. Not good. Thanx."

Very found no answer in her repertoire for this. She got into her car and drove home.

The house was quiet. And lonely. The sun had faded from the patio, but Very poured herself a glass of wine and sat outside, waiting for the darkness to creep in. She wanted to call Joey, but knew that she and her husband usually spend Sunday evenings in quiet time together. She finally went inside, turned on the TV, found some leftovers in the fridge, and sat in front of it, watching decades old reruns.

One show ended and Very punched the remote to 'off'. She got up and fetched the cigar box from her bag. She cleared off the dining room table and wiped it clean. Her hands eagerly held the box as she sat and placed it in the middle of the clean, empty space. "Notebook," she said out loud as she jumped up and retrieved it from the bottom of the bag. She opened it to a new page and labeled it 'Cigar box'.

"Slowly, methodically," she said. As a teacher would say to a student, a mentor to a mentee, a master to an apprentice. Everything in its time.

She opened the top carefully. The fall and subsequent snatch in Babe's front yard had injured the spine and now the lid wiggled and lay open in a lopsided manner. Very reached for the topmost photo. She realized then, that anything methodical was going to have to come on her part, as the photos had become jumbled in the melee. Perhaps a better solution was to sort them and put them in piles. On one side, she could put recent photos, those that had nothing to do with Danny and his past, and on the other side would be photos from the past.

Very carefully extracted a series of photos of Cassandra as a child. They were probably not the best photos, but extras, as Cassandra had said that she had taken the ones she wanted. When she came to one of Cassandra holding her own little boy, Very gasped. Cassandra might have been the same age as Frankie and the younger boy could have been Frankie at the age of four or five. The family resemblance was one of the strongest that she had ever seen. She set all these family photos on the left side. She took her notebook and wrote some notes about these photos. Now, she realized why Babe might have been hiding this box and the other photos from her.

If Very had seen these photos, she would have known immediately that Cassandra was Frankie's daughter. And that fact was something Babe wanted to hide. What had Cassandra said about when she was born? Just a month after Danny disappeared. So, that would have meant that she was conceived in the late summer. It was before Very met Frankie, but after Babe and Danny were married. So, did Babe have an affair with Frankie? Where was Danny all this time? Actually, it only took once, so it could have been an afternoon fling. Or was it something that started before the couple were married? One last fling with a former girlfriend?

She wanted to ask. Just to set the record straight. Or was it to find out if all of this was going on while she and Frankie were dating? The idea gnawed at her. A two-timer, getting a married woman pregnant and then a new girlfriend. Maybe that's why Frankie was so quick to say they should get married. If he couldn't marry the other one, because she was already married, then why not marry the one who was free to do so? Maybe the pregnancy was deliberate?

She chided herself. She hadn't asked about birth control, so whose fault was that? She remembered thinking that a few times without protection couldn't hurt. Or maybe she wanted to get pregnant? Was it some sort of romantic wishful thinking about the powerful pull of sexual passion? The results would be what they would be? Now, she began to feel the humiliation of a woman who was not the only one, not the first one, not even the most wanted.

"Stop," she said out loud to the photos on the table, the room, to all the thoughts raging in her head. "It was 37 years ago. Water under the bridge now. Get on with the plan at hand!"

She stood, walked into the kitchen and got herself a drink of water. The wine had made her thirsty and she drank greedily from a bottle of water. She returned and glanced at the box, inexorably drawn back to its contents.

She found some other photos of Babe and Danny Boy. There were twelve exactly, all taken on the same day. Ah, the twelve-shot rolls of film. Of course, they wanted to have them developed as soon as possible, so they took the whole roll. They wore the same clothes and posed separately, together and with a few friends. She peered closely at the friends. She turned the pictures over to see if someone had written anything on the back. A note on one of them, the best of the lot, was dated a year and a half before the disappearance. The others in the photos might have been Babe's friends, or her brothers, not the ones that appeared in the band photos. She put these into another pile.

She found old photos of groups of people in the garden, in various groups. They looked like the pictures that were taken when someone says, "Line up, everyone." And they do. A very young Babe in one, but the mature Babe she had met was so changed by age and illness that it was difficult to tell. Another few photos were of Danny Boy, including one of his senior pictures that she had already taken a snap of when she looked at yearbooks.

Very checked the stacks of photos and her notebook, making sure that all had been recorded, with dates, or the best she could guess if there was no other clue. She peered into the box. There were a few photos left, at the bottom. She couldn't leave them until the next day, that was not her way of doing things. She could never leave a little in the bottom of the box, one slice of cheese in the package, one cookie in the tray. No, she would finish the work, now.

She scraped up the few photos left. She put them in front of her. Why had they been at the bottom? Who had put them down under the old photos of Aunt Gertrude and Uncle Earl? Why had these been relegated to the bottom of the heap?

They were not the clearest, or best taken care of. Again, they were of that period when Babe and Danny had met, when photos of the 'band' had surfaced. Very looked at each one carefully, taking notes. Danny with Curly, Babe with Q-Ball, Danny with Q-Ball. Another one of the three band members together. A poor, underexposed shot of the three band members was one of the last. No wonder this one had drifted to the bottom of the box. Two more, along the same lines, were the last in the box. She turned them over. One said, "Trout's". The others had no writing. Very tossed them aside.

She repacked the box, starting with the old photos on the bottom. The photos of children didn't help her, and the series of Babe and Danny gave up no more clues. She separated them by interest to herself, checking to make sure that she had made simple notes for the ones that had only tangential interest.

Left until the last were the series of photos of Q-Ball, Curly, and Danny as the band. These she made sure to make careful notes about. When, who was in the photo, where it was taken. A few were taken outdoors, those were the ones that came out well, including the original of the three band members. The dark, indoor ones seemed to have been taken at the same time, maybe that evening or shortly thereafter. The hair length was the same and yes, the clothes were the same as well. The indoor ones, however, included some other figures in the back, in the dark. Other band members? Joe for one? Maybe. She looked closer, trying to see the faces hiding in the background, grainy, out of focus, shadows in the gloom.

One face, the white teeth glowing in the flash of the camera, swam out. She looked intently, then brought the photo closer to the light. The dark hair framing the face snatched at her consciousness, tugged and jerked at the threads of memories of that other face. She had had occasions to see that face often in the last weeks. And today, she had seen his daughter's face close up. She pinpointed the distinguishing features one by one, establishing the fact of what her gut had already told her.

This face, hidden in the obscurity of the three musicians at Trout's, was that of Frankie Monroe. This was it. This was the connection. She had her proof. Here was real, hard evidence that Frankie knew, and hung out with, the three guitar players in this photo. Q-Ball, Curly, Danny Boy, and Frankie.

Chapter Twenty-one: A Visit to the Hospital

The next morning, Very thought about going back to the Harger house in Tehachapi to check on things, make sure the paper got picked up and so forth. She wasn't sure the neighbors would do it. She also wasn't sure if Cassandra would have time to do that. Or maybe Cassandra had gone there to spend the night. Instead of going, she texted Cassandra.

She got a reply. "At Memorial" and a number. Presumably, a room number. What did that mean? Did Cassandra want her to come? Just for information? It was only a five or six-minute drive away, easy enough to run down the hill and check on Babe and Cassandra. What would she have meant by this cryptic text? If she would have wanted the new 'friend' to come, would she have said, "Come?"

Very took a few minutes to scrounge in a large box with leftover cards, 'free gifts' from charities, or her mother buying more than she needed or wanted, just to have a choice. She found a cute 'get well' card of kittens and puppies, signed her name and slipped it into a matching envelope. She hesitated to be overly familiar, but she couldn't address it to 'Mrs. Harger' or even Ruth as she had been told that everyone called her Babe. Babe it would have to be. Very neatly wrote 'Babe' on the envelope, giving it a cursory seal.

Very drove through the La Cresta neighborhood down to the hospital at the bottom of the hill. She easily found a parking place in the front lot. She entered the wide doors and stopped at the front desk. She checked that the number she had was indeed a room number. She had visited this hospital a number of times, but fewer and fewer as the years went by. People stayed in the hospital for only a day or two these days and then they were usually too sick to enjoy a visit. She got off on the floor that corresponded to the initial number of the three she had been given.

She felt nervous in hospitals. They were terrible places to pick up germs and illness was not something she enjoyed, hers or anyone else's. She stopped at the elevator lobby and looked around, trying to decipher the room numbers by the arrows indicating which corridor to seek. Regular rooms, specialty rooms, surgery and so forth. She spied Cassandra halfway down the hallway, standing alone.

Very walked towards her and then noticed her face was contorted with despair and misery. Tears rolled freely down her face, red with anguish. Very approached slowly, not wanting to intrude on her grief. "Cassandra?"

Cassandra turned her face to Very, not hiding any of the desolation. "She died, just now."

Ten minutes later they were in the garden room on the ground floor. It was full of large and small plants, and the light from outside filtered through their green leaves. Although the outside in Bakersfield ran more towards desert, cactus, mesquite or palo verde would have been more appropriate, the thinking that green trees and plants alleviate suffering was too well entrenched to buck the accepted protocols. Hence the stuffy, dark, smelling-of-humus garden was the go-to place for grieving families. It was supposed to soothe and comfort them. It was this or the chapel. So many people had objected to a sterile, non-denominational chapel, that the hospital committee had had this room built. The Green Alternative Peace Chapel. That was not what they called it, but they might as well have.

Very made Cassandra sit on a bench under a giant fern. "Tell me."

"They said to come back at noon and they would have paperwork for me. Thanks for rescuing me, I had no idea what I was going to do. I guess I need to call my sons, not that they could or would do anything. None of us are into death and funerals. My mom would avoid them at all costs. Only if she couldn't get out of it. She would promise to go, then at the last minute not show up. Paperwork. What does that mean?"

"Signing something. I don't think it is important or too difficult, just something that needs to be done. Tell me what happened. Last night she was still alive, and this morning?"

Cassandra wiped her face with a new tissue and took a deep breath, trying to calm herself. She blew it out with a 'woof.' "She seemed to be okay, or at least stable, last night. I stayed with her. She slept for a while; they had given her something for the pain. She didn't seem to be injured, except for cuts and bruises. But then again, she wasn't in the best of health. I went and got some food, talked to my oldest son, and then came back. She woke up and the nurse and I helped her drink a little, she had a dry mouth, although she had an IV. Anyway, she settled back down and then she tried to talk to me."

Very leaned a little closer in a gesture of empathy. "Did she know what she had done? Did she realize how dangerous it is to have a match with oxygen?"

"She knew. We had gone over that a number of times. I just don't know why she did it. I mean, half her problem was all the smoking she had done, but she really liked it. I figured that if she wanted to smoke, I wouldn't object, but I wouldn't help her buy cigarettes. I just tried to make sure that she had taken off the oxygen hose and turned it off. She didn't need oxygen all the time. Anyway, she didn't want to talk about that. I could hardly scold her at this point, could I? No, she wanted to talk about the past."

"Oh, I guess it was finding the body that did that, do you think?" Very chose her words carefully.

"I guess that was it. And then when you visited, that got her really excited, I think. She had met someone who had known all those people years ago. And I think she wanted to relive that time. She talked about the photos. She asked me if I had seen the pictures in the box."

Very leapt in with her own information about the box. "Oh, by the way, I have the box. You dropped it and I picked it up. I put it in my bag and forgot about it until I got home. So, there it is. I will bring it to you whenever you want."

Cassandra gave a gentle snort. "I don't really care about the box; she did. Like I told you, I got all the photos out of it that I cared about years ago. But thanks for telling me, I won't bother looking for it anywhere. Bring it back whenever you want."

Very licked her lips, a gesture she often used to delay her tongue blurting out things, a way to slow down the information while her brain had time to process. "You know, we didn't know each other at all, years ago. I didn't know Danny Harger, I didn't know your mom, I didn't know those guys in the band. Maybe I knew some people who knew them, but I didn't run in their circle."

"Hum. Anyway, she said she wanted to tell me about my dad. She said, 'I need to tell you about your dad.' Wow, I thought maybe she had some idea about how he died, about who murdered him."

Very leaned closer and said in a whisper, "You think she knew who killed Danny Harger? The other guys in the photo? Or maybe she thought it was my fiancé?"

Cassandra thought for a moment, "Or maybe she killed him?"

Very's eyes widened. "Oh, you don't think that, do you?"

"No, no I don't. I don't believe that at all, but it was something about the past and it was about those friends. She kept on, rambling a bit. She wouldn't say it exactly. Maybe she did think it was your fiancé who did it. She mentioned your name a couple of times."

"She didn't think I did it, did she?" Very seemed taken aback. She knew that she had not bashed Danny Boy Harger on the head and then buried his body in an orchard in Delano. But maybe Babe did. Or that Frankie had?

"Oh no, not you, but she said, 'That woman, Veree, she was his friend.' But you said that you didn't know my dad, so I was confused. Or rather, she was certainly confused."

"Did she mean that I was a friend of your dad's?" Very said this clearly, beginning to understand what it was that Babe was trying to tell her daughter about her father. "I think I know what she was trying to tell you."

"What, you know? How could you know? You just said that you didn't know them, so why do you know what my mother was going to tell me? Anyway, she got tired and confused and I tried to tell her it was okay. And then she went to sleep. There was a little couch in the room and I slept there. She woke up, but she never said anything else. I went for breakfast, and when I came back, she was gone. Now, I guess I'll never know."

"But I think I do. I think I know a secret, the secret she was going to tell you." Very reiterated her statement.

"You know something about my dad? A secret? Oh god, I hate secrets, no more secrets." She stood and made the 'Frankie' gesture, ending with the hand on her voice box. "If you know this secret, you need to tell me, now." Cassandra's anger blazed across her face, a sudden storm of hard outrage and passion. "Who are you, barging into my life, into my mother's life? My father, found dead and buried in an orchard, and now my mother, blown up by a stupid machine that was supposed to keep her alive. And you have secrets. It's just not right. You tell me, tell me now!"

Very shrank back into herself. Only twice had she encountered this kind of flash of annoyance; quick, volatile and seemingly springing from deep displeasure. Frankie stood to be angry, shouting his annoyance. It vanished quickly, but was surprisingly swift and abrupt.

"Sorry," Cassandra said, sitting back down. "I have a tendency to blow up when I get excited. I always have. It's something I've had to try to squash all my life. I'm a little emotional right now, and I have the right to be, but I shouldn't be taking it out on you." Cassandra breathed another deep inhale, and slowly let it out, closing her eyes and taking control of her emotions.

Very was impressed. Obviously, Cassandra had learned to mediate between the emotional volatility of her inner self and the socially accepted protocols of expressing displeasure. "Maybe it's better if we do this later. You have enough on your plate right now."

"No," came the swift reply. "It's all part of it. My father being found, after all these years, my mother dying this awful death. If there is a secret, I want to know. I'm grown-up, I can take it on the chin."

"I wish your mother had told you something. I know very little, not how or why, but maybe when. Oh, I think this may be too much right now and I don't have a lot to tell you. In fact, I was hoping to talk with your mother, hear what she had to say. I mean, maybe not today, when she was injured and all, but later. And now..." Very stopped. "I wish she had told you something. It's not really my place. But maybe I am the last one. Maybe."

Cassandra looked at Very with narrowed eyes. "Just tell me. Say it. My father wasn't my father? My mother wasn't my mother? I'm not who I think I am?"

"Why would you say that?" Very looked at Cassandra with alarm, afraid of the volatile pique she knew lay underneath her now pacific exterior.

"I am right," Cassandra muttered in a small voice.

"You knew?" Very matched Cassandra's voice in volume, a sibilant whisper.

Cassandra turned to look at Very. "I didn't look like them, either of them. I didn't look like my cousins, I didn't look like the family portraits. None. I looked like me. And I know that we can look different from our parents, that genes aren't absolute, but I always thought... And you know, when you're little and you're angry, you say things like, 'I'm adopted, aren't I? I'm not like you, you're a horrible person' to your mother?"

Very tried to stifle a smile. She knew the drill. "Yeah, I understand."

"So, once she got really funny about it. She yelled back, 'Yes, you're right, you're adopted, you're not really part of this family. What do you think?' And, of course, I got really scared, because I didn't have a dad, I only had my mom. And if she rejected me, what would I do? And then she said, of course I wasn't adopted, what a silly thing to say, blah, blah, blah."

While Cassandra had been telling this story, Very had been rifling in the depths of her bag. The envelope had become slightly crumpled, but the photo lay within, safe and whole. She took the picture out of its mismatched shell and handed it to Cassandra.

"Just to let you know, I'm not sure, really sure. But, you tell me. Do you recognize this man?" Very said this kindly, knowing what a punch this was likely to be.

Cassandra's face transformed from sad and distressed to puzzled and excited. First, she touched the face that was so much like her own, tracing the line of his broad forehead, down to his snub nose. She caressed the freckled skin on his cheeks. She touched her own strong jawline and then rested her hand on her voice box. "This is my father?"

Very glanced down at the photo and then directly into Cassandra's amber-flecked eyes. "Your eyes are just like his, and your voice, that kind of always a little hoarse voice, that's his too. So, you tell me what you think?"

"Who is he?" Cassandra once more studied the picture. "Is this your fiancé?"

"Yes. And I think he's your father. His name is Frankie Monroe. And he disappeared 37 years ago; the same night that Danny Boy Harger did."

Chapter Twenty-two: A Visit with Joey

That afternoon, the heat gathered in the southern end of the Valley, baking the hard gravel ground into earth harder than cement. A breeze sprang up, but only stirred the dust into devils and coated what little green remained with a patina of khaki.

Very and Joey were finishing their late lunch in the cool of the shade in Joey's backyard, when Joey demanded that Very tell her exactly what had happened at the hospital.

"After I showed her the photo, and told her his name, she said nothing. Not a word. She stared, she caressed, it's the only word that fits her actions, the paper, his face. She looked at me for something, what, I don't know. Confirmation? I mean, the only other people who know what really happened are dead or have disappeared. I knew nothing about all of this until yesterday, when I saw Cassandra. I guess we'll never know, unless Frankie shows up. Maybe those other characters in the band know something. It's hard to tell what anyone knew. The way Cassandra told the story of her mother teasing her about being adopted, I mean, that was weird. But we all go through that at one point. Usually it's because we don't want to be part of that family. And I am pretty certain that Babe Harger is, or was, Cassandra's mother. But I am just as certain that Frankie is her father. And the fact that Babe, in her last hours, tried to tell Cassandra something about her father. Well, in the end, I had to pry the photo out of Cassandra's hands. I'm sure she wanted to keep it, but it's the only one I have. The only one. And, whether I loved him, or if now I hate him, I do not want to let go of it. They called her to sign the papers, so she had to go. But we have each other's numbers. So she can call or text anytime. I told her that I'm available if she wants to talk some more. She certainly has plenty on her plate right now. This thing can wait."

"If it can wait, why didn't you let it wait? I mean, at this point in her life, her 'father' having been found after all these years, her mother blowing herself up, now learning about, or at least being introduced to the mystery of her biological father... Very, why didn't you keep this to yourself for a few more days? Or forever? What difference does it make?" Joey spoke with the force and conviction of one who knew she was right.

"Maybe you're right. But she did try to tell me that her mother wanted to tell her something, and the way she phrased it, it was this secret. But I guess maybe it would have been better just to let it lie for a few days. It does seem selfish of me to blurt out my secret knowledge. I did it for myself, because I couldn't keep it in any longer. There, is that what you wanted to hear?"

"Yes," Joey answered. "You are usually so kind and generous, that when you're not, it comes as a surprise. Is this really going to throw her off her stride? Did she seem upset about Danny Harger being found? That's one thing. If you have always thought that your dad had disappeared and you had never seen him, had little feeling for him, to find out that he had been murdered before you were born, what can that do to a grown woman? And then, her mother, wow, that would have been a blow! But it sounds like she was not in the best of health. So, wouldn't you have to think of someone like that dying? When your mother got old and frail, what did you think? Did you think about her dying?"

"Do you remember how stoic I seemed? Not a tear? It wasn't that I didn't care, it's just that I had gone through it all in my head so many times, that, in the end, it was anticlimactic. It was as if I had mourned her for years, or had been preparing myself for her demise. It was frankly a relief when she went. And then, oh, I halted my life. I kept telling myself that I would clean up this and that, that I would throw all her clothes away, that I would send all those ugly knick-knacks to Goodwill, but nothing, nada, zip. I felt paralyzed. So, maybe Cassandra feels the same way. And, this idea that her father isn't her father, a blow. It's off my chest at least. I am not going to hide it from her, like the others did. Oh Joey, my life is so complicated, I don't know how to handle it!!"

"With dignity, peacefulness and calm," Joey said. "I am also part of your life, you know. We've been through too much together to sever each other from the fabric of the other's life. I'll do what I can. And that includes telling you the truth when you're being a bitch. So, what else happened?"

"Oh, I still have the cigar box. I picked it up from the lawn in front of the house. I'm keeping it safe. And snooping. But I found a photo that I think proves that Frankie was in the gang, the band, if you will. Obviously, all the photos and newspaper articles don't show him or mention him, except in an oblique way, so he must have been only a hanger-on. But there he was, in one photo, so I know that he was in the group. And that means that he knew Danny Boy and presumably his wife. They were all mixed up together. And I didn't know any of them." Very shook her head.

Joey leaned over and patted Very's knee. "It was a long time ago. How were you supposed to know?"

"I was engaged to be married. It was my job to know, to find out what kind of a man he was!"

"You were in love!?"

"What is being in love? Not even in lust. Just so happy to be normal, average, to have what other girls had. A guy who liked me, wanted me, treated me well. No, scratch that last one. But I was happy."

"So, let's leave it at that."

They sat in amicable silence, each immersed in her own burdens.

"Joey, I know that this is a difficult ask, but does your hubby, the sheriff's officer, know anything? Can you ask him if he would tell me what he knows?"

Joey let out a wail. "Very, you know he can't say anything."

"Yes, he can, if it is public. Just let me know if he knows anything before it comes out in the paper. That's all. I mean, what good is it being married to a man who knows all the dirt on all the city and county officials and you can't find out in advance?"

Joey laughed. "I know, I know. I'm always telling you the news before the newspaper, but I don't think that this qualifies. I am sure there is an investigation that has lots of secret angles to it, but I can't ask him to tell me who they are investigating or anything. You know."

"Yes, I know. But I can still ask. So, what else is he good for?"

Joey looked at Very sideways. "Why marry a man younger than yourself if not to make sure that he still has energy in middle age? When we met, and he is still seven years younger than me, it seemed like being a cradle robber. Now, it is no big deal. No one seems to notice at all, least of all us. But he is still virile."

"Humph." Very snorted. "Well, I'm off to see the PI. I have some more to add to the story and maybe I can dig into some more databases with different information."

"So, how's that going?" Joey perked up.

"The PI or the databases?"

"The PI."

"Great. We seem to get along just fine after that little rocky start. He's actually a very funny guy in that sarcastic and self-deprecating way that some men have. You know, like the ones who are self-conscious and shy, so introverted that you almost expect them to refer to themselves in the third person? I get him."

"Married, girlfriend??"

"Joey, haven't I told you what he looks like as well as his personality? He's the male equivalent of 'old maid'. He's a bird watcher and a solitary type. I understand. You need to overlook the weird bits and he's a good guy."

"Wow, I never thought I'd be in the middle of such a fantastical problem. I know my hubby gets involved in these things all the time, but never me personally. But here I am, best friends with the left-at-the-altar, connected to the body in the orchard and now, a new-guy-in-your-life lady of the year."

"You are such a hoot, Joey. See ya."

Downtown, she easily found a space to park as it was close to quitting time. She knocked on Darrell's door and listened for his response. Not hearing anything, she reached for the doorknob. Suddenly, it opened and Darrell stood in the office, a slow smile spreading across his face. "Hi, I didn't think you'd make it in today."

"Well, I did. I have some things to tell you. I guess maybe I should have called before I came knocking?"

"Here," said Darrell, his hand extended. In the palm was a newly made key, with a whistle attached on a key ring. "Yours."

"Wow. Thanks. And a key ring with a whistle?"

"It's one of those old-fashioned things, a lady needs a whistle in case she's attacked. And it's always there on your keychain. I thought you'd appreciate it."

Very smiled. Should she feel offended for being thought of as a 'helpless lady' or flattered that Darrell was so thoughtful? She went with a man with a heart. "This is very kind and considerate. Thank you. And it reminds me that I really should call before I come. But as I've said, I have some illuminating evidence for the case."

Very filled Darrell in on the events of the past two days. The return visit to the Harger home, the discovery of Cassandra, the daughter born a month after Danny Boy had disappeared, the spitting image of Frankie Monroe, the explosion, the retrieval of the cigar box, the perusal of the contents and the finding of the faint photo of Frankie, the death of Babe Harger in the hospital, the revelation to Cassandra of her presumptive father, all tumbled out, but in order and with sufficient detail. Very told the story with the help of her notebook.

"What a story. You came in here looking for your long-lost boyfriend. I thought it was going to be a long shot, maybe an off-chance discovery, but basically a big dead end. Instead, look what you've found! I've never seen such a coincidence, or maybe it's good detective work. In any case, hats off to you. Where do you want to go next? Any ideas, intuitions? Or maybe you are clairvoyant?"

"Hardly second sight. But my gut tells me that Q-Ball and/or Curly might have some ideas. We need to see if they are still around. I did find some addresses, but they were hardly the 'own this home' type of places. And the latest was at least ten years old. But they stayed around Bakersfield, even the criminal stuff was here. Maybe they've left town, I think I'd be tempted to do that, but…"

"If they had family here, you can bet they didn't stray too far. Even if they aren't nice enough to give you a place to stay, they are always good for the odd $10. Family guilt. And the thought of jail, well, maybe they'd bail you out?? Anyway, it's an off-chance, but look into the addresses. And the other thing, the photo, or photos and newspaper articles? This one, for example." Darrell called up the file and quickly clicked on and enlarged on of the later photos of just Q-Ball and Curly. "See, this was taken at Trout's. You know, the old guys still hang out there. They may know something. It's still a well-known place and I'm sure it's just full of leads, if you know who to ask."

"Have you ever been there? I haven't. I'm not sure how to approach it." Very looked again at the photo.

"Well, have you read the section in the book about interviews and interrogation? It could help you strategize your questions, prepare the methods of approach, figure out what hidden weapons you may have."

Very abruptly stood up. She had had a revelation. She had initially come to Darrell to pay him to do this for her. She had no idea where to start, and her method of doing things was to get an expert to do what you couldn't do yourself. But now, she knew. It was not what Darrell was going to do, or even what 'we' were going to do. This was her case now. She would make decisions, she would call the shots, she was in the driver's seat and success or failure rested with her.

Chapter Twenty-three: A Visit to Trout's

On the way home, Very first thought about telling Joey her plans for the evening. But just as at Darrell's office, she changed her mind. She needed to look within herself and make her own decisions. Her mother was fond of telling her to 'paddle her own canoe,' so she straightened her back and prepared for her night out at Trout's.

First of all, she did look at the book again and the chapter on interviewing and interrogation techniques. She reviewed the ideas on preparation for the interview, that is, knowing all the facts, getting witnesses on your side by looking for common connections and of course, taking copious notes. This last piece of advice was for criminal cases, in case of being called to court, and she had no intention of getting involved in a legal case. Or was she going to get involved with a court case? No, she was only looking for Frankie, not going to get involved in anything else. Then there was the suggestion of recording the interview. She could do it on her phone. But then again, maybe not.

First, she needed to prepare. So, what should she wear? She went to her closet and slid back the door. She was presented with a rack of middle-aged woman clothes. Cotton shirts, matching pants and a few skirts. Her sweaters and winter things were in the back, but Very thought that she didn't have any 'cowboy' outfits among her winter offerings either. She pulled the door open further and pushed her head into the depths. She found a leather vest and pulled on it, causing the surrounding clothes to tumble to the closet floor. Damn.

"Okay, leather vest. Now for some jeans." She opened a drawer where she kept her pants. Gardening pants, shorts, three-quarter length, then a pair of skinny jeans. The newest and latest from last year. There was embroidery on the legs, roses winding up the side seam. It was the best she could do. No shit-kicker boots, but how about some low-heeled shoes that were easy to dance in? Good enough. A belt, she needed a belt. And she remembered why she almost never wore the skinny jeans with the rose embroidery. They fit so low on her hips that she needed a belt to hold them up. Aha, she had a belt with a genuine cowboy buckle. It was an advertisement for a drilling company, not something she would normally wear, but perfect for this. She laid her finds out on the bed, and tackled the drawer where she knew the belt should be. Finally, she assembled her cowboy outfit for interviewing old Country Western singers at Trout's.

She carefully painted her face with what make up she could find. She was never one for 'painting', but had enough of the proper kind to appear like an aging Dolly Parton. Then she washed it off and tried again. She checked herself in the mirror and decided that she needed a colorful bandana or scarf around her neck, to set off the plain white blouse she had donned. Should she dig out her grandfather's ancient Stetson? It had never fit well, so maybe she shouldn't go the whole hog. She found a small bag that hung from her shoulder and could fit her money, keys and a small notebook. Copies of the photos were folded and tucked inside as well.

She sat and waited. When could she reasonably expect people to be at Trout's on this Monday evening? Certainly by eight. Possibly by eight. If she went later, would she miss them? If some were off to work in the morning, wouldn't they just come by for a drink and a few songs and then leave? But then again, she was looking for the old farts, those who might very well be retired and so stay out later. Or maybe so old that they wouldn't visit the place on a Monday evening?

At seven-thirty, Very stood to go. She thought what kind of drink she could order to make it stretch out without getting tipsy. But she still needed to appear worldly-wise, so a Diet Coke wouldn't do. Beer, lite beer. But did she have enough in her stomach to counter that? She didn't want to have to order bar food to soak up the alcohol, so she dug in the fridge for a hunk of cheese, which she ate swiftly.

At eight, she judged the time was ripe. She drove to Panorama and made a left turn, to head downhill. The hilltop park still had a line of cars parked on the curb and she could see figures walking and jogging in the faint light of the western sky. She saw a few bobbing flashlights, but most walkers used their night vision. She really should get out there more often, she chided herself. She had not been pursuing her daily workout since the body was found in the orchard. One dip in the cool pool had been the extent of her bodily exertions.

She kept to the right lane as Panorama Drive split and she took the downhill curve to Manor Drive. She crossed the Kern River and noted that it was dry. After all, it was mostly dry these days, the only time it carried water was in the spring for a few weeks or maybe months in a wet year. Really, this was a desert. All the green trees and grass could not disguise the fact that before man began pumping water from the ground, the only year-round green was along the river courses. A bloom of green appeared every winter and spring when it rained, but by April, the hills had turned to the washed-out yellow of dry grasses.

Very took the Roberts Lane exit and a 270-degree offramp brought her to the top of the bridge. From here, she had a view of the bluffs. They stood out against the twilight, stark steep hillsides that rose from the river at their base. The lip was unstable, yet some still wanted a house perched on the edge with a view of the oilfields. Most of what she could see was taken up by Panorama Park, a thin strip of land with a paved walking path and a few trees and bushes, many that had been there since the WPA work done during the Depression.

Suddenly, she was in Oildale. The sidewalks were absent or only token patches of cement, cracked and clogged with weeds. It was an autonomous suburb of Bakersfield, originally settled by the Okies and other southerners and Midwesterners who came to work in the oil fields. Pronounced 'Awldale' by the locals, its most famous son was the Country Western singer Merle Haggard. Although he no longer lived in Bakersfield, he had put it on the map. He maintained that he still loved the place, but privately, many said he hated Bakersfield and openly said he would never live there again. Abandoned cars were more abundant than higher on the hill, and bicyclists sped down streets, invariably with no lights and in the wrong direction. She slowed down, keeping watch for malfeasant cyclists. It was the poor man's transportation, but she resented the cavalier way they rode.

She turned right onto Chester Avenue and glided north. Not much traffic, so Very went slowly, watching for the neon sign of the dancing trout on the opposite side of the wide street. When she saw it, she pulled over and parked where she could see the front door.

Trout's was housed in a characterless one-story building on the west side of the street. The only thing that distinguished it from its neighbors was the sign. It read, "Trout's, cocktails, dancing." It had been variously described as a redneck karaoke dive bar and the last of Bakersfield's legendary honky-tonks. Whatever it was called, it looked like Oildale.

She had a good view of the front door, just under the iconic sign. No one came out, no one went in for the fifteen minutes that she sat, patiently watching. What was she waiting for?

Then a group of girls appeared as if from nowhere. They sauntered up to the door, stood and straightened their hairdos and clothes. Two of the three had curls and beehives, straight out of the 70's and reminiscent of Dolly Parton. One wore white short shorts and another had a miniskirt matched with a leather vest with loooooong leather fringe, draping far below the length of her skirt. The third wore tight jeans and high heels and wobbled as she walked, hampered by the constricting nature of the jeans. They opened the door and Very could hear, from across the street, the thump-thump of music and the cackle of laughter. Just as the girls were going in, two young men came out. The group stood at the door as they exchanged greetings, flirts, barbs and teases. One of the young men wore a Stetson, so big that it threatened to cover his ears.

Young people, hanging around the open door. Soon, they separated and the girls went inside, the young men outside, to lean against the building and smoke a cigarette.

Was it time? Enter the bar and try to question anyone who might know the band members? She started to rehearse in her head what her opening lines would be. The young men reentered, and she heard the noise again, urgent, insistent music and peals of hilarity. Why weren't more people coming and going? There were only the three young girls who had gone in the door, and it sounded as if the bar were full. When did they get there? She had been parked in this spot, watching the door for almost half an hour. Yet the bar seemed full.

She saw someone appear from the darkness along the side of the building. Ah, a back door. There was a large parking lot behind the low buildings and it stood to reason that most people would park their cars there and enter and leave through the back door. Should she do that, rather than leave her car here and cross the street? She thought and the more she thought, her breath began to come in irregular noisy sucks and exhaled in throaty coughs. She felt a dizziness descend. Stuck behind the wheel, she couldn't put her head in her lap to stop the feeling of faintness. Instead, she hung her head.

Thump! Very felt and heard the noise that came from the rear of her car. She lifted her head to look into the rearview mirror and she saw two blurry faces staring at her.

"Ack." Very sat up, startled and frightened.

The thwack was repeated and accompanied by a loud wailing scream. Very felt the car move as if someone had pushed down on the bumper or climbed onto the trunk. She looked again and saw one face smashed against the back window and the bare backside of another person.

Very started the engine and released the brake. Her hand hovered over the gear shift as she assessed the situation. Then a face materialized at her window, only inches from her face.

The man had a scanty beard, as if he was unable to shave or too young and immature to have much hair. His hair stuck out and wafted in the evening breeze. His mouth, deeply red and surrounded by yellowed teeth, was open.

"Yaaahh." The sound was high pitched, aggressive and sinister.

Primal fear invaded her brain. She put her foot to the gas and the car leapt away from the curb with a squeal of tires laying rubber. She did not look behind her, but swerved out into the right-hand lane. A thud accompanied her leaving the parking space. She heard no more as she raced ahead up North Chester Avenue.

The light was red, but she didn't notice until halfway through the intersection. A swift prayer went through her head that no other distracted drivers, hopped up cyclists or hovering police were nearby as she made her escape. She turned right at the next intersection and sped through the dark streets. Night had fallen and the streetlights were dim, missing and spaced far apart. When she approached the looming oil tanks on the east side of Manor Drive, she slowed, switched on her indicator and without much thought, turned right and drove quickly towards the bluffs and home. As she neared the tight exit turn to Panorama, she slowed down so as not to go flying off the road onto the river banks below.

As she pulled into the driveway of her mother's house, she wished she had left some lights on. Darkness and fear had transformed the middle-class house in the suburbs into a haunted lair of demented and deranged psychopaths. She fumbled in her bag for Darrell's keychain with the whistle.

Chapter Twenty-four: Searching the Databases

The next morning, she had regained a calm exterior. Maybe. She, at least, had slept well.

She leaned back in her breakfast chair and encircled her coffee cup with hands that threatened to shake. If she recalled her mad dash away from Trout's bar, her heart began to beat faster and a fog to develop. But when this happened a few times during breakfast, she took a deep breath and closed her eyes. She could then dispel the evilness. She also thanked the gods, trolls or fairies of silly ideas that she had not discussed the aborted trip to Trout's with anyone. Nothing had happened. Nothing at all. Except for a few millimeters of rubber burned from her tires. End of story, a bad idea that had never happened.

Who were her tormentors? She knew they had nothing to do with her current inquiry. They were just crazy Oildale kids. Maybe high on drugs, or drink or the excitement of being a young male. They had found a person out of place, and had taken advantage. The attack, for that was what it was, was not dangerous. Her windows had been up, the doors locked, no glass was broken, and no damage was inflicted onto her car. She had no reason to worry or fear that she would be targeted again. The only thing she had to fear was the lingering sense of unease, the victim's burden of dread and suspicion. She would not succumb!

She was torn. Her mother's piles of clothes, old letters, keepsakes and just plain junk called to her. She had repeatedly urged Sissy to claim her inheritance, but there had been no commitment, yet. No one in her family had been a fast starter, swift off the blocks, and so expecting it now seemed unwise and fruitless.

Going back to the office, Darrell or no Darrell, was certainly an idea that created more enthusiasm. Split the difference, she decided.

She grabbed her keys and headed to her car. She folded the back seats down in preparation for piles of supplies for removal and storage. Boxes, lots of boxes, different sizes and styles, for the mounds of stuff that would reside in them.

The parking lot of Home Depot seemed full for a Tuesday morning. She parked as close as she could get without getting too close to an oversized pickup truck or outsized SUV. A sedan seemed a puny car to drive in Bakersfield where the standard for a household was: a pickup truck, a family van and an SUV. The size of families in Bakersfield was not substantially larger than other parts of the country, but a plethora of vehicles was de rigueur for any self-respecting middle-class household. What could a man drive to work but a truck so large that he needed a ladder to get into the cab? How was a family to travel en famille to visit Grandma unless it was in a big van complete with individual TVs? Any self-respecting housewife, off to do her grocery shopping in a small car? Never! An SUV meant that she could hold her own on the freeway, sitting high and powerful in her gutsy car. She could buy a month's worth of groceries with room to spare for the always-in-the-back toys, sports equipment and emergency kit for earthquakes.

Very entered the store and stood not far from the entrance, trying to establish which aisle she needed to cruise first. Her outsized shopping cart was not going to hold what she needed, but she had to start somewhere. She headed for the back of the store. As she rounded the corner on Aisle 5, three kids careened past her. Why they weren't in school? Was it a holiday, or maybe one of those 'teacher' days they had too many of (in the minds of parents), or too few of (in the minds of administrators), or just too annoying (in the minds of teachers)? As the three disappeared from sight, she heard a commotion that carried their voices high into the rafters.

As she continued down the aisle, she looked to the right and left, checking out products on the shelves. Suddenly, a cart appeared in front of her, blocking the aisle. A display had created a narrowed, tight passageway, but the woman and her companion in front of her completely blocked the passage. The woman sat in one of the complementary electric carts, and directly behind her was a similar sized person, obviously, a daughter or sister. They were enormous. Pale in color, hair twisted back into thin unwashed ponytails, they were clad in matching lightweight cotton shorts and shirts that billowed around them. They must have had a difficult time just getting into the store, not to mention getting around and choosing their purchases. They walked with difficulty, breathing stentoriously. They had stopped.

Very backed up and went through another aisle. The enormous problems of obesity in the region were being presented graphically to her. Her daily life was either blithely getting into her car or walking wherever she wanted, but these women had severe challenges. She knew herself to be lucky.

She found the section she needed under 'Storage' and stood dumbfounded at the offerings. She loaded up her cart with cardboard and plastic goods and headed for the checkout counter.

Boxes filling the back of her car, she headed home. When she arrived, she unloaded them. Buying the boxes was enough for one day. She called Darrell and then immediately headed downtown.

Seated in 'her' chair, Very discussed the possibilities of finding Q-Ball and Curly and what databases she could use. Pointedly, she neglected to mention the previous night's ill-fated visit to Trout's. Darrell did not mention going there again. He, too, must have realized the futility of that avenue of inquiry.

"Oh," Darrell said. "I forgot to tell you. I'm off to Woolgrowers for lunch with the insurance guys I work with. Would you like to join us? Not much shop talk, but maybe it would be good networking if you could meet them? How about it?"

Very looked at Darrell's eager puppy dog look. She couldn't disappoint him. "Sure, why not? As you say, good networking. And who doesn't like Woolgrower's?"

They discussed databases for another few minutes, then left in Darrell's car. The ride to East Bakersfield was swift, just over a mile as the crow flies, but a stark change in ambiance. Trash skittered around the streets, piling up in the gutters. A feeling of being left in a time warp when everyone else has moved on hung over the streets. The neighborhood had not changed since her childhood. It was always the wrong side of the tracks, but now it seemed like a movie set for some dystopian fantasy film. A few pedestrians strolled the streets and she knew that when the light faded, the drug dealers and prostitutes would emerge to engage the hapless inhabitants of the down-and-out residential hotels that dominated the neighborhood. Once, it had been the center of the Basque sheep herding community and a few restaurants still remained. The rest of the Basques had made good and lived in the better parts of town, but no one could resist slumming to come to the restaurants.

As they entered the side door, Darrell was greeted with loud whoops and backslaps by two men his age. They greeted Very, introduced as Darrell's new colleague, with unctuous phrases of welcome. She knew she was being sized up for the ability to help out with investigations. Somehow, she felt rejected as insurance investigator material, but acceptable as a secretary. She shrugged it off. This was Bakersfield; many years behind in social justice, racial and gender equality, and a lot of other things. Darrell's colleagues were nice guys, with unfortunate political and social views. They all liked the food.

"What'll you have to drink? Picon punch? Or does that have too much punch for you?" one said to Very.

Taking it as a challenge, she consented. She liked a Picon punch, but not usually in the middle of the day. It was the splash of brandy at the end of the making of the cocktail that tended to hit Very too hard. One before lunch would be all right. She hoped.

They had gathered in the bar and as soon as their drinks were ready, their table was too. As soon as they were seated, light crusty French bread in a basket was slapped down by a harried waitress. The rattle of dishes, plates and voices vibrated in the air as hungry patrons ordered, ate and talked their way through course after course. Soon, a tureen of vegetable soup, heavy on the cabbage, appeared and was followed by a round plastic bowl of salad. The salad contained mostly large chunks of iceberg lettuce with a decorative touch of tomato, but it was also covered with a thin layer of oil and a faint smell of vinegar. Crimson red chile sauce, thick and chunky, and boiled beans, both in shallow serving dishes, appeared on the table, the rims already covered in the sauce. She debated whether to use her napkin to wipe the sauce off the edge, or just dig in and lick her fingers. The four dug in, handing the plates around family style. They ordered. She chose the garlic fried chicken, the men had steaks. As they dug into one dish, another appeared. An oval plate of spaghetti, lightly covered with tomato sauce with a hint of hamburger meat, and another plate of long yellow French fries, still sizzling with hot fat from the fryer, made their appearance.

When the plate of pickled tongue arrived, there was a grab for it. One of the insurance men was polite enough to ask if she wanted any, with the smile of greed hovering around his moist lips. Very shot back, "I'll certainly take my share, but if anyone else wants to decline, I'll fight you for the rest!"

The insurance man howled with laughter and politely took only his portion. "You can always tell the real lovers of Basque food by who will fight for the last slice of pickled tongue."

Darrell poked at the thin slices of fatty tongue, swimming in oil and vinegar, and then passed the plate on. "You can fight over my portion," he whispered to Very.

Very laughed and only took what would have been one quarter of the slices. She had no intention of fighting the bulky men if they really wanted the fatty meat.

"Hey, did I ever tell you about the guy I met in the restaurant in Reno?" said one of the insurance guys.

"Yeah," answered both of the other men, in resigned voices.

"Tell Very," said Darrell. "She was born here."

"You were born here, really? That's unusual. Anyway, you should be able to give a good answer. So, this guy asks, when he found out I lived in Bakersfield, 'Which is better, Woolgrower's or Noriega's?' It seems as though he asked everyone, but hadn't bothered to find out for himself. So, which do you think is better?"

Very chewed and swallowed a French fry. She paused for deliberation and then opined, "They are different. Not better, just different. The atmosphere is so, so, so… distinctive, individual. The food is much the same, but they each have a particular ambiance. Can't say." She forked another rapidly cooling piece of potato.

"Here we go," chirruped the waitress as she lowered the enormous tray she carried to the edge of the table. She handed around plates of meat, and they started on this course.

Although the insurance men finished their steaks, both Darrell and Very elected to take most of their meat home. The plate of blue cheese looked too inviting to pass up and she carved off a piece, pressing and smoothing it over a small piece of bread. The tang finished off the meal. The men paid for her lunch and thanked her for being an interesting lunch companion. She went away puzzled. Was she supposed to take it as a compliment or as a comment on her feistiness? She was too old to change herself.

Back at the office, Darrell started by checking his emails and then turned to Very. "Can I help you with any databases? Show you how to work anything? Give you pointers, ideas?"

"I think I want to take a nap. But in reality, I just need to go through more of these same databases for other states, not just California. I haven't tried all the variations on Frank. And I also haven't tried different spellings of Monroe, or variations of that name. There's a lot in front of me. Just slogging hard work. Thanks."

The two turned their backs to each other and got to work on their separate machines. Even though she had initially thought she wanted to sleep, the work enthralled her. She found a Frank Monroe in Pennsylvania with a birthdate just two days off of her Frankie's and her heart began to race. In a few moments, she had a photo, and then she relaxed. It wasn't her Frankie. She inhaled and let out a long noisy sigh.

"Trouble?" Darrell asked, startled at Very's breath.

"No trouble. Unless you call a dead-end trouble. I have searched and searched. I have tried different spellings, variations on names, I've looked everywhere. I haven't covered the whole country or other countries, but I have found many Frank Monroes. The same ones, over and over. They are real, they are listed on voter rolls, licenses and so on. But not mine. My Frankie Monroe isn't here." She gestured at the computer, indicating the knowledge within. "My Frankie Monroe is not around anymore."

Darrell stared back at Very. "Unless he has become someone else entirely."

"Or dead." Very had come full circle. The body in the orchard wasn't Frankie, but could he be in the same condition? In another orchard? At the bottom of Lake Isabella? Or?

Chapter Twenty-five: A Chat with Father Sullivan

At 8:30 the following morning, Very got a text from Joey, "Come for coffee?" Very texted back, "10ish. I'm cleaning out now."

She had decided to start the morning with things to throw out or give away to charity. That would leave less for Sissy to go through. She gathered big black garbage bags and began at the bottom of her mother's closet. Slippers, sandals, shoes, high heels (?), even an old pair of mukluks erupted from the bowels of the closet. Why would anyone want these worn, aged, broken-down, and dirty-with-garden-muck shoes? She saved two pairs of high heels for the Goodwill bag, and put the others aside for the garbage. Maybe she could recycle something? On further inspection, most of the shoes were bought before the age of recycling, and besides, NO one recycled shoes.

She pulled open the bottom drawer of a large double dresser that her mother had had as long as she could remember. The drawer was sticky and hard to open and when Very had wiggled it open, she realized why. It was low down and in later years, her mother was unable to bend down. If it had become sticky, then a further reason not to open it. What was in it? Treasure or trash? She vowed that she would not leave the house today until she had sorted this one drawer.

An hour later, Very straightened from her position on the floor. Two piles lay on either side. She found the half full bag of discarded shoes and scooped one pile to join the dross and dregs headed for weekly pickup of trash. For the other mound, she found a box and tossed it in. Cards, letters, newspaper clippings, lists of friends in various clubs, all that might be useful. She doubted that one-tenth would remain after another go at it. She looked at the clothes hanging in the wall-to-wall closet. Why do we have so much closet space? If we do, we can always find something to fill the space. Better to have less space and fewer clothes. Who would want this collection of out-of-date, torn, stained, holey, poorly mended cheap clothes? Throwing them all away would do the world a favor.

She washed her hands, three times, trying to wash off the dust and stains of years. Finally, she gave up and went to Joey's house.

At the front door, Very rang and called out. No one answered, so she let herself in the unlocked door. Out in the backyard, Joey had been joined by her daughter-in-law with the newest baby. Very felt obliged to bend over and chuck the drooling infant under the chin and admire the burbling baby.

She sat down and sighed. Extolling the virtues of little ones and venerating them as treasures of the family was something she had always found difficult to do. She had feigned interest all of her life, not letting any residue of disappointment show in the public face of Vermilion Blew. Inwardly, she had also suppressed any thoughts that she had missed out on one of the ultimate joys of life –

motherhood. Joey tucked the baby onto her hip and bounced it, cooing like a proud pigeon mommy.

Very sat back and watched. Obviously, part of her disdain for the delights of motherhood was the loss of her own baby. Unplanned, and hardly anticipated before it was gone. She never even knew the sex. Was it that early tragedy that made her dislike the smelly little humans, or would she have had the same standoffishness with her own? Would she have been a good mother? All women must hope they will be good at parenting, but she knew that many women felt cheated out of their own lives by the devotion expected towards their offspring. Men rarely ran the same risks; they could be themselves and still be fathers. Because so little was expected? Being a father was easier? She thought her own father a good one, and she had hoped that Frankie would have embraced that role well. She would never know.

Very watched and listened to Joey and her daughter-in-law. The younger woman wanted some advice about how to deal with a member of some committee who was constantly nay-saying. Joey asked a series of questions, trying to get the daughter-in-law to phrase the contentions in more neutral terms, trying to get her to answer her own questions.

Very wandered inside, helped herself to coffee and skipped the cookies. She felt fat and bloated from the day before. Outside, the conversation had turned to the neighbor across the street and the barking dog. Very fidgeted for another ten minutes, then looked at Joey with a quizzically lifted eyebrow. Joey mouthed a 'sorry' and Very mumbled her goodbyes to the gathering.

"I'll walk you out to your car," Joey offered, jumping up from her seat, and handing the baby back to its mother.

At the curb, Very turned to Joey. "Does your daughter-in-law do this often, ask your advice?"

"Yeah, a lot. She doesn't always get along with her mother, and I take it as an opportunity to build bridges. Good relations. Sorry about the tête-à-tête not happening."

"Don't apologize. You have such a great way of giving advice, I hope your family values that. We can talk another time. Nothing much has been happening, no more news since the weekend."

"Actually, all I wanted was to give you this." Joey handed Very a small square of cheap notepaper. "From the deputy sheriff."

"From your husband?"

"I can't say where it came from." Joey stood tall and answered without the smirk that Very knew lay just below the surface.

"Okay, I get the message on where it came from, but what…?"

Very unfolded the paper and read the cryptic missive. "Talk to Father Sullivan."

Very drove directly to the church. Although she was not a member of his congregation, everyone in Bakersfield, and many beyond, knew Father Sullivan. He was outspoken, he was involved in the community, he was a character larger than life. He was also a large man, now running to the fat of late middle age. And recognizable from the many photos that appeared in the local paper. In fact, she thought there might have been one on the back side of the original 'body in the orchard' story.

Very parked in the parking lot, along with a dozen other cars. There must be a church gathering, a bible class, a cleaning brigade, or something special to bring all these people to the church on a Wednesday. Very walked in through the large doors at the top of a shallow set of stairs. The vestibule was empty except for the various stands that held the weekly bulletin and announcements of future special events, mission appeals and such things. She walked further into the main part of the church. The hush was the familiar quiet that was demanded in the House of God. She came here with her Dad as a child. They hid out at the back, but occasionally when she was very young, she was directed to the two front pews to sit with the other kids. There, the nuns watched the children's every movement and used their unnaturally long arms to physically chastise unruly or just plain antsy miscreants. She could feel the pinch on the back of her neck as she walked down the main aisle towards the front of the church.

Father Sullivan stood in the middle of the main aisle talking with a group of older women who sat in the 'children's' seats in the first two pews. Very walked closer and took a seat some rows back and listened in.

She soon zoned out on the chit-chat of the group and tried to find a good memory to reminisce about. Confirmation and graduation sprang to mind, but the only thing she could definitely remember were the clothes she wore. A pink hand-me-down dress from her cousin. A full skirt with crinkly itchy fabric for the flouncy slip to make the dress poof out for an effect. That was for confirmation. She had scored a new dress for graduation with a matching pillbox hat. She tried to picture herself wearing such outlandish items these days. But they must have been important for her, since she recollected the day wearing them with so much more clarity than the actual 'solemn' events. But the events took place here, in this church with the high stained-glass windows, the marble floors and the lingering scent of incense.

Father Sullivan finished his part of the meeting and sauntered down the aisle towards Very. She stood to greet him. "Hi, I'm Very Blew. I've been sent to you."

He erupted in a throaty chuckle and indicated that he and Very could move further away from the group, who were continuing their gathering.

"Who sent you? And, most importantly, why?" They sat in a pew towards the back.

"I'm looking for someone," Very began, ignoring the first question. "Or rather, I'm looking for a number of people who might help me find who I am looking for. And I was led to believe that you could help me."

"So? Who are you looking for?"

"I'm looking for Frankie Monroe. He disappeared 37 years ago. But he had some friends, that apparently are still around, who might have some information about him."

"I don't know any Frankie Monroe, but who are the others?"

"Q-Ball and Curly, otherwise known as Stanley Leon and…"

"Glenn Wilson. Yes, I know them." Father Sullivan sighed.

"Well, of course you know about the body in the orchard?"

Father Sullivan breathed deeply, "Yes, Danny Boy Harger. Finally found. But what does this have to do with Frankie…?"

"Monroe. They apparently were in a band together, before Frankie and Danny Boy disappeared. Do you know anything about that?"

Father Sullivan laughed again. "A band. Boys, playing at playing guitars, playing at singing, playing at being grown-ups, or at least what we thought were grown-up things. We went to high school together. I knew them and maybe I hung around with them, trying to create music."

"I saw some newspaper articles that talked about Curly, that he had a voice like Johnny Cash."

"Yeah, he had a voice like Johnny Cash, low and rumbling, raw even. But he couldn't sing. He could growl and say the words, but there was no music in it. And Q-Ball was better than the others on the guitar, but one guy strumming couldn't carry them very far. No, they didn't go very far as a band. And they might have gone a little further in their career, such as it was, if they weren't such mean bas…" He stopped and looked at Very with a face of pain. "You see, they were not nice. Neither of them. Curly had a mean streak that would come out very unexpectedly. He's got a scar, right here," Father Sullivan pointed to his cheek. "He got into a fight one night at Trout's, someone broke a bottle and used it on him. Lots of blood and a nasty deep cut. When he gets angry, that scar turns purple and ugly, as if it remembers the insult. He's had a hard life; two wives, two divorces, I don't know how many kids. Too many jobs, but none for long. And his family doesn't speak to him anymore."

"He's that despicable?" Very looked startled.

"No, actually he is a very calm person most of the time. When I used to visit him in prison, because of course he landed there, more than once, he could go for months without a single foul word and behavior to match. He's had a lot of friends over the years."

"You visited him in prison?"

"Part of my ministry. And when he is an old acquaintance, even more important. They left school, note how I didn't say graduated, and went on. I went to the seminary. But I ended up back here, in Bakersfield where I began and it's hard to ignore a former classmate in need."

"And Q-Ball?"

"Q-Ball? Similar, though much more of a loner. He never picked fights like Curly, just got mixed up in them. And he stayed away from entanglements with women, though that didn't mean he didn't like them, just that he couldn't attract a good woman to settle down with. And he wasn't mean, or really violent. He was in prison for embezzlement, writing bad checks. And as for getting a job, well, he did work as a handyman, often trying to cage a place to live in exchange for labor. He could be a real charmer when he put his mind to it. But the unfortunate lack of hair put people off. You know, everyone called him Q-Ball. He'd meet someone new and tell them his name, and say 'call me Stan', but then the new acquaintance would find out, and he'd be back to being Q-Ball. "

"What about Joe or Jose?"

"Yeah, he was one of the gang. He died about five years ago. He had diabetes and then had a stroke. In years past, it was always heart attacks that got men at that age. Now, it's obesity related illnesses and cancer."

"Were there any other men that hung around the band that might have information? What about someone named 'Killer'?"

Father Sullivan snickered again and deflected the question. "Oh no, no one named that, not involved."

"So, do you have any idea where I could find Q-Ball or Curly? I still think they may know something useful to me." Very gritted her teeth in frustration at this conversation. Thumbnail sketches of the past lives of peripheral characters didn't seem to be getting her further along.

"I just saw Q-Ball's social worker last week. I think I know exactly where to find him, but let me talk with him first. That's just because he may need some help with a conversation about the past. He's in a rather delicate state. And I can ask him about Frankie Monroe. But let me have a few days, okay?"

"What about Curly? Do you know where he might be? How can I get in touch with him?" Very pushed the growing frustration from her voice.

"That's another matter. He may be more difficult to find. No fixed abode, if you know what I mean."

"Homeless?"

"That's about it. In some ways, it's better for the rest of society. As long as he can get his disability check and has some food, he's probably better off alone. The last I heard, he had a tent pitched down below the bluffs. I'm sure if you went looking for him, you'd find him. I think he still has that head of curly hair, so everyone would know him. You'd better take someone with you."

She felt a sigh emerge. At last, some real information.

"And what was your interest in Frankie Monroe?"

"He left me at the altar. I thought I'd gotten over it, but when the body was found, I thought it was his. But I was mistaken. But then I found out that he knew Danny Harger and probably the others. And so, I think that 'the others' may know something."

"About Frankie and Danny?"

"Yeah. Where Frankie went. Where he might be now."

Father Sullivan was silent, waiting for her to give some more information, justification for her search. Or was he tired of the conversation?

"Are you sure you want to know?" he said, ending the conversation.

Chapter Twenty-six: The Bluffs

Very stood on the top of the bluffs looking down onto the river snaking below her. She hitched her small backpack off of one shoulder and pulled on a small waist belt that was tucked into her elastic-waisted shorts. She turned the opening to the front, unzipped and took out her phone. She tried Darrell's number again. "Damn, answer, you," she said to the phone's face as the screen indicated that no one was answering. As she had already left a message, she decided that a second, or was it a third, message was not going to be necessary. Father Sullivan's advice burbled up. She waited for a few more minutes, scanning the area.

Behind her was the path, ten feet wide in most places, well asphalted and planted on both sides with trees that eventually would provide shade, and grasses and bushes that could withstand a shortage of water. When she was young, it was a field. Tall palm trees and some other trees had been planted. A few had survived the years of neglect. There had been a road, out to this point, and on Friday and Saturday nights, there was always a line of parked cars, their noses pointed to the north. The oil fields had been there for far longer than the path and their lights lit up the fields in an eerie nighttime display of otherworldly luminescence. As a child, she had called the refineries 'fairy castles.' Parking on the bluffs and watching, or not, the oil field lights was called 'counting oil wells' and her dad insisted that it had been going on as long as teenagers had cars.

Now it had been gentrified and no cars were allowed. Even skateboarders and bicycles had been banned from the wide walkways. It had become a family area, with joggers, families, dogs on leashes. Once she had been walking early in the morning and had become irate with a fellow walker for not having his large, loping dog on a leash. She had started to yell at him, when she realized that the dun-colored canine that was loping alongside the path was a coyote, not a domestic dog. She had stopped and watched the wild animal, so accustomed to humans that he ignored them on his turf, and then he walked quickly away, down over the bluff. Near this same spot, she had seen a great grey heron down a wriggling squirrel, headfirst. The bird had gulped and gulped. She had watched fascinated as the fluffy tail disappeared and the heron's neck had bulged and bulged as the tiny mammal descended. She hoped the bird had not gotten a stomachache. Many times, she had seen the Kern County Rescue services using this section of the bluffs for training. As rugged as any mountain gulch, this area was much closer to home and more accessible to cold water and snacks for the trainees.

Very looked down at the series of trails that led off the bluffs to the bike path below. They spilled off the edge like rivulets, brown in a sea of golden grass, snaking their way to the bottom. Some zigzagged, others plunged at an angle that was worse than any roller coaster, and much less fun to traverse. At the bottom were two moving bodies of water. One was the canal, the other was the river. The canal flowed when water was allowed out of the dam for irrigation. The river flowed when it rained or there was too much water in the dam. At this point they ran parallel, the canal closer to the bluffs, the river a few hundred yards north. Someone had told her that jackrabbits lived on the north side of the river and cottontails on the south. Urban legend most likely, but she had never seen a jackrabbit on the bluffs, only colonies of the fluffy-tailed variety of lapins.

Beyond the river were the oilfields. They stretched as far as one could see, disappearing in the smoggy distance. Pumpjacks rose and fell, the refineries belched smoke, and fires lit the tall smokestacks at night, burning off impurities. The blood of Bakersfield was black smelly oil. Her family, and the families of so many of her acquaintances, were strewn with men whose first job was in the oilfields. They wore hard hats, jeans stiffened with oil, gloves stained and discarded. Hands were scarred, missing fingers, and some were permanently sidelined with injuries. For many, there was no choice but to go to the oilfields for work. The only true way out was education. She had devoted her professional life to trying to make that escape possible for as many as she could persuade to stick it out to graduation. And then she steered them to college, hoping they could envision a life in a field other than using their hands picking fruit or turning greasy pump handles.

As Very tried one more time to get Darrell on the phone, she looked behind her at the walkers on the bluffs. It was still very warm this late in the afternoon, even for September. A hot wind blew, occasionally creating swirls of dust that rose from the river bottom and sprinkled fairy-dust like debris on all those who walked or jogged on the path. There were so many of them, she did not feel alone. Forget Darrell, lots of people around.

She chose a path that was steeply down, but not so precipitous that she would trip over her own feet. She stopped three-quarters of the way down and took a sip of water from her water bottle. She unbuttoned her shirt, glad she had thought to wear a sleeveless shirt underneath. As she neared the bottom, she glanced around. There were always the marathoners, the ironmen, who lurked around the bottom of the bluffs, ascending as fast as they descended. She heard voices nearby and relaxed. No, she wasn't alone. As she hit the bicycle path, she cautiously looked both ways. She walked close to the edge, but took this asphalted way as it was much easier and flatter than the paths on either side of it. She pricked her ears for the sound of bicycle tires on pavement.

She crossed the canal on the bicycle path and then entered an area scattered with trees and bushes. Trails led off in all directions. She turned around, trying to get her bearings. While she did so, two cyclists whooshed by, their heavy breathing louder than their tires, neither of them more than a murmur and a hum. A dog barked in the wind; she couldn't tell which direction it was from. A series of whinnies alerted her to the presence of horseback riders, accompanied by snippets of conversation, snatched by the wind. What was it she was looking for? A tent? An encampment? A wandering person to ask? What would she ask?

She headed down one well-trodden path and immediately scared a covey of birds. They flew into the air with a whir of wings, and faint whimpers of alarm, swirling above her in a controlled pattern of flight. She walked down towards the river, the path curving away from the bicycle path until she could no longer see anyone if they came or went.

Then she saw the tent. It was tucked up under a tree, but the bright blue gave it away. She slowed her pace and approached, on guard. Two young men, wearing dirty torn jeans and tee shirts lay lounging on a blanket on the ground. Their skin was burned brown by the sun and the distinctive smell of marijuana was in the air. They sat up and looked at her, smiles exposing mouths not seen by a toothbrush or a dentist in a long time.

"Hi," she said with more confidence than she felt. "I'm looking for someone. An older guy, named Curly. Do you know him?"

One guy leered at her, his sickly smile exposing broken teeth. It was not a nice smile and a little voice tried to tell her this was not the best idea. But she stood taller and took on her authoritative demeanor, a theatrical trick honed by years of working in Bakersfield high schools.

"Who wants to know?" the second man said.

"My friend. He's related to him and wanted to check up on him for the family. He's with me, asking around. We were told that he was camping out down this way."

"Why should we tell you?" the first one said with anger in his voice.

"Why not tell her? Are you jealous? Someone maybe has something good coming their way?" the second one grumbled at his friend. He turned to Very, "Is he the guy with all the hair, needs a haircut? Probably full of lice?"

"His real name is Glenn, but everyone calls him Curly, because of his curly hair. Sounds like him," Very replied. "Where is he?"

The second man stood and she tensed. A trickle of sweat rolled down her back between her shoulder blades. Was it the heat or fear?

"Yeah, I know where he is. He's down that way, in the big grove of trees. He chucked out the prostitute who used to be there. Mean bastard. She had a good thing going, and everyone knew where to find her. Then Curly decided he wanted the place to himself."

"Which way?" she asked, stepping back out of the campsite.

"That way," the man flung his arm in a wide gesture towards the left, up the river.

She turned to leave, but kept an eye on the vagrants as she went back the way she had come.

The first man who had spoken stood and shouted as she quickly left. "Tell him he could share that space. He doesn't have to be so mean to everyone. We could all be there."

Very walked quickly until she was out of earshot and sight of the campsite. She stopped and took a deep breath. She slipped her backpack off her shoulder and dug out her water bottle. She took deep gulps, spilling liquid down her shirt. She screwed it shut and then reached again for her small waist pack. She took out her phone and tried Darrell's number again. There was no sound of ringing, no sound at all.

She looked at the screen. "No service," it read.

She looked towards the bluffs in front of her, now deep in shadows as the sun began its descent. Then, she remembered someone once complaining to her that cellphone service was spotty down below the bluffs. Not in line with the towers, and who needed the service there anyway?

Chapter Twenty-seven: Curly

Very stood with the phone in her hand while she thought of her plan of action. The phone was of no use, so put it away. She did so, tucking her shirt in over the small pack with her house key, phone and photocopies of driver's license and medical cards.

She had used the 'friend' before when presented with men who threatened to get out of control. She had learned that if you say 'friend' and 'he' with confidence, the lie is more acceptable. Maybe it would have been better if she had waited to contact Darrell, but so far so good. Why not plow ahead? She was closer than she had been at any time in the past few days. The former addresses of family members or ex-wives were nowhere near as close as this. The men had definitely identified Curly. All she needed to do was walk down this way and when she identified the place, she could come back later, with reinforcements.

She listened to voices in the distance, female voices, laughing, and she felt more at ease. She swung her arms as she walked down the path. At her feet were the marks of horses, some dog paw-prints and a set of boot prints. She was not alone.

Ahead was a copse of tamarisk trees, looming high above the trail and all the other bushes and trees around. What did the young man call it? A big grove of trees. Of all the landmarks around, this was the only one that fit that description. She walked with careful steps towards the trees, and then saw the opening. Someone had hacked out an entranceway on one side of the thick tangle of bushes so that a narrow tunnel-like passageway led to a clearing. She bent over and looked through to the other side, where light poured into the spacious camping ground. "Hello," she called. She realized that she still gripped the water bottle in her hand. A weapon?

"Hello," she called again. "Hi, I'm looking for someone. Curly, Glenn Wilson. Glenn, are you there?"

Suddenly, a figure appeared at the end of the tunnel. Wild gray hair streaked with bits of the original brown greeted her. Under the dirt was a deep jagged scar on his cheek. The thin figure wore numerous layers of shirts; the pants he wore had never seen the inside of a washing machine and thin cloth shoes graced his feet. His short beard was like his hair, streaked brown and gray. He smiled a toothy grin, although all his teeth were stained brown.

Very hesitated. "Curly?"

"Must be, huh? Whaddyathink?" he growled.

"Hey!"

"Who are you? What do you want?"

"A friend said you were here."

"You don't look like no social worker. They don't come down here, even though they know this is where we live. They don't bother making house calls. So you're not a social worker. So, what friend do I have that is looking for me?"

"I am. A friend of a friend. I thought maybe you could help me." She still stood outside the short tunnel and spoke loudly to Curly as he stood at the other end of the leafy entranceway.

"Ah well, if you are a friend of a friend, you had better come into my lair. My casa is your casa." He backed off from the entrance and made a grand mock bow indicating she should enter.

Very slowly made her way through the thicket walkway and entered the circular site. There was a tent, campfire pit and a bag hanging from a long limb that gave shade to the spot. It looked like a bear bag, but why? Who could imagine any bears this far from their mountain homes? It was also out of the way of a lot of other critters who might want to rob poor campers and the homeless of their food. A section in the back was obviously the trash heap as it gave off an odor of decay. Curly stood his ground near the door of his tent.

"So, what do you want?" he stuck out his lower lip in defiance.

"Information."

"About what?"

"I'm looking for someone."

Curly took one step forward and looked out from underneath his mop of hair, "Who?"

"Frankie Monroe. I'm looking for Frankie."

Curly laughed. "He's gone. A long time ago. I know nothing about it."

"But you know when he left? How he left? Where he went?" Could it be true that she had finally found someone who knew Frankie and knew something about his disappearance?

"Who wants to know? It's a long time ago. Who cares?"

"I care. I want to know. Frankie and I were going to get married. And he left me at the altar. And now, now you tell me you know something about it."

"Years late. Too late. You came all this way, just to hear that he is long gone."

"Well, I only live up there," she used her head to indicate the bluffs, not visible from the enclosure, but still a landmark.

"It's too late. Too late for Frankie." Curly shook his head and the jerky movements began to tell her something. Drugs? How much? What kind? Upper or downers?

"Where did he go?" she demanded, using her clear and concise teacher's voice.

"How should I know. But I know this, lady. He owed me."

"He owed you what?"

"Humph. He was a wrong 'un. He cheated me; he cheated a lot of people. You should thank your lucky stars that you got away."

She stood still and waited for more information. Curly knew Frankie and knew that he had gone, had disappeared. He knew more. She could feel it, and feel his reluctance to tell more.

"How'd you get involved with such a loser? You look like you have more sense than that? What could you have wanted with him? Pretty boy looks, got any and every girl he wanted. Always wanted more than he deserved."

"He was a charmer too, you know." She needed to defend her lost lover. Or did she?

"Yeah, he was. Charmed everyone. Wormed his way into our little band for a while. But he wasn't really into it. He couldn't play, couldn't sing. Useless. Ran him off, we did. Told him to go find another couple of suckers, we weren't having it."

"Who's we?" She knew the answer, but she needed to hear it. The more information she could get out of him, the better.

Curly sat down on his dirty blanket spread in the dirt, in front of the tent. "Q-Ball. Me and Q-Ball. We were the band. We were the only band. 'A voice like Johnny Cash.' That's what they said about me. 'My name is Sue. How do you do.'" Curly sang, or rather said, in an excellent imitation of the tag-line of Johnny Cash's most famous song. She listened to his voice, and had to admit that his 'growl' was like the famous singer's.

"What do you know about Danny Boy?" Very asked.

"Harger? Naw, don't know nothing about him." Curly snorted in derision. Both Curly and Very knew this was a lie.

"He disappeared," Very said simply.

"He did. He did that."

"He disappeared at the same time that Frankie disappeared."

"You don't say! Well, Hallelujah and bring on the fireworks. So, what does that have to do with me?"

"You knew both of them, didn't you?" her voice took on a harsher tone. She was tired of all this silly chit-chat.

"Maybe I did. So, what does that tell you? All these years ago? Who cares?" Curly's tone rose in anger to join hers.

"But I'm looking for Frankie. I want to find him."

"When you find him, what then? What are you gonna say to him?"

"I want to know why he left."

"And you think I know that? Naw, Frankie is just a side track."

"What about Danny Boy?"

Curly stood and faced her. "I told you. I don't know anything. Those two, Frankie and Danny Boy, they were bad eggs. Not worth nothing. Useless to us, useless to everyone. And not worth looking for, that's for sure."

"What do you mean, useless to you? In the band?"

"The band, the band? Don't you get it? Don't you know nothing? That was a front for the real dough. The real thing. We could go anywhere, talk with anyone, and we had our cover. We had our places, our people. Crappy Danny Boy! He wanted in on it, he wanted to spoil everything. He had no idea what to do, what we were doing. He just bumbled around, scaring our customers off. He was a BIG liability. You know that big word? You know what it means? Sure you do, you and your fancy talk, you probably have a nice education. So, what were you doing with Frankie? Another loser, another bum. What did you want with him? Slumming, huh? Liked the bad boys, huh? Good looking, with all that fancy combed hair and his flirty smiles? He had all the girls, believe me. They all loved that Frankie. He couldn't help that they threw themselves at him. They'd see him at the bar and go dancing right up next to him, wiggling their backsides at him. He got you, didn't he? I'll bet he did. You and half the other girls in town." Curly laughed, a cruel taunting laugh.

Very cringed. Her unplanned pregnancy. Cassandra Harger, with Frankie's face. Her own experience on that last fateful day. Curly's words were doing their work, plunging like knife blades into her ephemeral memory of the laughing, playful, warm-hearted Frankie.

"That Frankie, he shoulda disappeared himself sooner. But you know what? He's not worth looking for. I'd just be thankful he left when he did, if I was you."

"What about the others in the band? Joe, and Killer? Did they have a part in all this?" She knew very well that Joe was dead, but Killer?

"Ah, Joe. Good guy, but misguided, shall we say. Misguided all around. He had nothing to do with anything. And that Killer. What a wuss. Holier-than-thou. All the time, telling us what we should be doing. 'You should be doing this and that. Where's your pride, man? Where's your COMpassion? Who's your brother's keeper?' Naw, Killer is out of it. Way out of it. You need to keep away from him. He'll lead you astray. Nooo, he can't tell you nothing. Won't, either." Curly fell silent, and closed his eyes, as if he was ready to nod off.

Did she need to push him to keep him talking? She searched her brain for something that would keep him babbling on. It had all been vague, nebulous, pie in the sky, unrevealing, and in the end, he was not giving anything away.

She decided to provoke him, "Where's Danny Boy?"

"How should I know? He just left. Got out of town. Probably." Curly sat down again, tired of the conversation.

The light in the middle of the copse began to leave and the edges of the sky to blur. The mood of the conversation darkened with the sky.

"They're not worth looking for, even if you could find them. Garbage, both of them." He looked sideways at Very. "You're never gonna find him."

"How do you know?"

"Because I made sure that when he disappeared, he would be gone forever. I got mine back. I got mine." Curly's head lolled and he laughed. A laugh that was half cry.

"They found Danny Boy." She looked closely at Curly to see what reaction he would have to this news. Obviously, he had not heard. "Didn't you know?" She could not refrain from throwing in this last barb, taunting the drug-addled homeless ex-con at her feet.

"Where? Who found him? What are you talking about?" Curly tried to sit up, but had trouble, slipping back onto the blanket. He slurred his words. "What do you mean?"

"The body in the orchard. Last week. They identified it. You didn't know?" Her words came out sharp, nasty.

Curly stood, his face ugly with anger. "What?" he roared. "What did you say? In the orchard? Who told you that?" Spittle flew from his mouth, which had turned into a dark, monstrous hole, spewing hate and profanities.

He lunged at Very, growling and screaming, "...name is Sue. Now you're gonna die!"

Very turned to leave the copse. She felt her small backpack being ripped from her shoulders as she bent down to get through the opening. She also heard a roar of rage.

Her voice froze with fear, but not her legs. She willed them to take her out of this place of untimely confessions. There was a children's book, 'Run, Rabbit, Run.' She was now the rabbit. She ran.

Chapter Twenty-eight: Run for Your Life

Very felt a weight on her back, but it was only the other strap to her backpack. She let it slip off her shoulder, buying her some time. She winced as the dying sun shone directly into her eyes, momentarily blinding her. She stumbled forward, hoping she remembered where the road was.

The wild crazed man in the copse campsite had grabbed at her; he had threatened to kill her. And he had confessed to the murder of Danny Boy Harger. Now, he had a very good reason to kill her too. And she needed to get away from him. She had never been a runner. She was a swimmer, a walker, and an occasional jogger. Her hiking boots weren't the best for running, but they would grip the ground and support her ankles. But did she have the muscles, the strength to outrun this man?

She heard another roar behind her, and curses. "You won't get far, you fat old lady! I have your stuff, I'll catch you, I'll find you. I'm gonna kill you. You won't get away from me!"

Very, spurred on by these threats, ran blindly down the road. As she came to a shadier spot, where she was out of the sun's burning rays, and could see, she briefly turned to face her foe.

The sight frightened her and put energy and force into her escape.

Curly stood tall, made taller by his massive head of hair, a swirling gray and brown halo that he shook like some fearsome predator. He gripped her daypack in one hand, held out like a prize, an item of booty, taken from the war. His mouth drooled and he spit with every word. Like a komodo dragon or a gila monster, his saliva held as much poison as his words. He roared with anger and frustration. "Come here, come and get your itty-bitty pack. Your treasures are inside, aren't they? I'll find you, don't worry. You can't run away from me."

Very only took a few seconds to check one more thing. Did he have a weapon? She saw no sign of a gun, or the glint and shine of a knife. But that did not mean he didn't have anything more dangerous than his fists.

He lunged forward again and Very turned towards what she hoped were the bluffs. Within a few feet, the path turned again and Very had the choice of the sun in her eyes, or running away from the bicycle path and the way out of here. She hesitated. Then she heard the sound of running feet on the soft sandy ground immediately behind her. She glanced over her shoulder and shuddered at the sight, only a few yards from her, of the crazed Curly throwing himself in her direction. She chose the path where she could see, but immediately thought it was the wrong one. She noticed that it veered away from the bluffs. But the option of 'sunlight in your eyes' was not the right one either. Which way had she come?

She plowed ahead. She forced her feet to keep to a pace that was difficult with her boots. The ground was soft, sandy and gravelly by turns. Her feet felt like they were being dipped in cotton balls, and every time she lifted one, the other sank some more. She began to tire, her throat burning with thirst. The footsteps behind her came closer.

The road curved around again until she hit a T-section. One headed to the west, with the orange bright sun still burning low in the sky. The other headed to the east. This time, she could see the bluffs directly above her. She stopped. She hesitated. She listened for activity, for other people. Where had the horse riders gone? Where were all the hikers? Which way should she go? Which way was more direct? Which way was easier? She thought of the two bridges across the canal. Where were they? The one she wanted should be just in front of her on the left. Or was it to the right? The other bridge was much farther away, up towards the mouth of the canyon.

Behind her, crashes through the undergrowth alerted her to her pursuer. Curly burst from the brush directly to her right. He must have taken a short-cut. Of course, he would know all the trails here. He screamed in triumph, his hair swirling in the air. He still held her pack and he waved it in triumph. But he didn't have her.

She turned to the left and ran again. She heard Curly behind her, his heavy breathing and his muttered threats. But his breath came easily, unlike Very's. "Run, Rabbit, Run," she said in an attempt to keep up her energy.

The path narrowed. Branches now swept into her face and body, causing her to slow and stumble. What happened to the wide path? Had she taken a turn she wasn't aware of? She stopped and looked around. Just behind her was the drug-crazed Curly, still running, still holding her pack.

"Aha. You thought you could get away! But you're in my neck of the woods now. I know this place, and you don't. You can't get away from me."

A small window of time and space opened to her right. If she could carry on down in this direction, she should come to the canal. It couldn't be far away. She stuck her left arm out in a great sweep, and raced through an opening in the brush she had given herself.

Caught off-guard, Curly dropped the pack. As he bent to pick it up, Very threw on a spurt of energy and ran some more. Soon, the trail petered out. Ahead was a field of small, immature bushes. Hearing the man behind her, Very plunged ahead. She leapt over the small bushes and pushed her way through others. Her legs, encased in shorts, screamed at the scratches. She gritted her teeth against the pain. She felt the presence behind her, but knew better than to stop to look. One large branch reached out towards Very and she pushed against it. As she forged ahead, she let it snap back into place.

A shout behind her let her know that she had won one round at least.

She could see clearly now and the bridge over the canal lay ahead and to the left. The bluffs loomed in the evening sky. The shadows carved deep into the gullies, leaving black scars and sharp ridges. Very wanted to see if she could see any late hikers, but she dared not stop. She ran on, trying to listen for any runner behind her, but was unable to hear for her own heavy breathing.

Finally, she reached the bridge over the canal. She had a clear view in front of her and she knew that when she got to the bridge, it would bring her back into the view of bicyclists and hikers.

Clang, clang, clang. Her boots hit the bridge. She struggled on to the half-way point and stopped. With her heart in her mouth, she turned back. There, only twenty yards away, was the crazy man, still holding her pack.

He stopped at the beginning of the bridge and Very could tell that he, too, was winded by the mad run. He opened his mouth and a noise, a half-roar, half hiss escaped. Very saw his brown, broken teeth and shuddered. A wolf chasing his prey.

"Run for your life," she said in her head, not wanting to expend any more wind or energy talking now.

A series of walking paths branched off from one another in a vein-like pattern. Ahead were the main paths that led to the top of the bluffs. To go straight towards the main path would be difficult and not easy at a run. To take one of the many deviations would lengthen the journey.

She headed straight for the nearest large path that headed upwards. She had to leap over some rocks and a small gulley slowed her down. But soon, she reached a wide path that led upwards. It was one of the major trails, with wide switchbacks. Longer, but easier.

Very looked back. She could see no one, hear no one. But she knew he was there, somewhere. He didn't act like he was going to give up so easily. She turned and started up the trail. Head down, breathing deeply and evenly she pushed herself into a power-walk.

"WAAHH!" Curly stood in front of her, not twenty feet away. "Thought you had lost me, huh? No way, Curly is still here. You are dead meat! I'm gonna get you. I'm gonna…"

Very didn't stop to hear anymore. She turned right and took a minor trail that appeared to go straight up. No switchbacks. No soft trail. Rocks slipped out from under her feet. She heard grunts behind her. But here, her boots did as they were meant to do. They crunched into the rocky slope and helped her climb up.

The trail rapidly deteriorated, but Very knew that it was only two hundred yards up to the path on top. She put her head down and climbed up. Soon, she found herself on all fours, using her hands and feet to climb the cliff.

"Awww ouch!" Very's hands landed in the middle of a tiny patch of cactus, with paddles smaller than the size of her hand. Densely crowded, they pointed their long sharp spikes straight up, keeping her hands from finding a clear spot. She darted sideways. Three long drags brought her to a spot above the patch of rare Bakersfield cactus. Gritting her teeth against the pain of the few spikes that had found her, she rested one knee in the dirt. She heaved a deep breath.

A vise bit into her heel. A muffled growl of triumph came from behind. Curly pulled her heel, causing Very to lose her balance. She toppled to the side and over onto her back.

"Argh," she said as loud as she could. She twisted her heel, trying to free it from the crazed grip of the man pursuing her.

She dug her backside into the dirt of the steep hillside. "No," she screamed. "No, no, you are not going to get me!" She lifted her other foot and pushed. It met air.

"I'll get you. You will not get away from me. I'll make f***ing sure you won't get away. I'll kill you too." He snarled and growled like an angry dog.

She reached down with both hands and tried to free her foot from the vise. The pain of the cactus spikes hampered her. "No," she screamed again.

She lay on her back and lifted both legs into the air. Swiftly she kicked out and down. She repeated the move. Again. And once more. The last kick met a hard body part with a crunch. A barely muffled cry let her know she had hit a soft spot.

As soon as she felt the vise loosen, she turned over and started up the hill again.

Behind her she heard a screech of surprise and pain.

Cautiously, she turned and peeked behind her.

Curly was down in the shadow of a trench. Made by the runoff of the few rain showers that gave enough water to move the dirt, these gullies were perfect spots for a few plants or bushes. Curly was caught in one. The one with the small hands of very spikey cactus.

"Arghhh. I'll get you, I'll kill you. You won't be able to hide. I know you!" he screamed in pain and frustration.

Chapter Twenty-nine: Joey Rescues Very

She scrambled harder, ignoring the pain in her hands, the deep scratches in her legs, the throbbing tiredness in her thighs and arms. She listened to the screams and curses fade behind her.

Suddenly, she came to the wide winding trail that she had left below to take a short-cut. Without glancing behind her, she took it. She ran, heaving and now she noticed, sweaty with her exertions. She needed to get away. Because now she knew, and Curly knew, that he had confessed to murder.

Very thought briefly of what Curly wanted to do to her. He wanted to do the same thing to her that he had done to Danny Boy Harger. He wanted to bury her in a wild place where no one would ever see her again.

Where were the hikers, the walkers? She had not seen or heard anyone since she began running. She scanned the trail ahead and saw no one. Then she noticed that the sun had set and the evening darkness was falling rapidly. "Go for the top!" she urged herself.

Abruptly, she was there. People walked on the path, two joggers ran by. Very found a large tree and sank down with her back to the river, hidden as much as possible from the view at the top of the bluffs.

Another jogger, his bare chest sweaty, ran by. He glanced in her direction, gave her a weak smile and ran on. She must not look too bad. The jogger had acknowledged her, but hadn't stopped to ask how she was, if she needed help. Surely, he would have if she looked worse. She looked at her hands. Tiny smudges of dried blood oozed from where some of the spikes had pierced her palms. She grabbed one still sticking out and yanked. Blood came out, deep red.

She pulled herself to her feet. She knew she was not out of danger yet. She fumbled in her tiny waist pack for her phone. Now that she was back in the land of connectivity, she stabbed at Joey's number. She waited until she heard Joey's voice, then continued walking. She tried to force herself not to look back.

"Joey, I need your help. This is really serious. Meet me at my house as soon as you can. Sooner. I need you or someone to come now. NOW!"

She heard Joey assent to the request and then she put away the phone.

She looked back over her shoulder. The good light was gone. Murky shadowy figures moved along the path. Sweat streamed into her eyes. She could not afford to stop and look, she needed to get away.

At Panorama Drive, the traffic sped by. It always sped, even when it was rainy or foggy or walkers wanted to cross from one side to the other. Hardly stopping to gauge her run across four lanes of speeding traffic, Very looked both ways, then ran. She heard tires squealing and a car honking. She didn't care. As soon as she gained the south side of the street, she swiftly walked to the corner.

She glanced over her shoulder. Figures walked in the park, a few were running.

Were they joggers, or her pursuer? She stayed close to the curb and ducked into the alley. The narrow roadway was deserted, but Very kept to the edges, near the garages and fences that lined the alley. She tried to keep as quiet as she could, but still maintain a good pace.

Suddenly, a light went off over her head. Damn those motion sensor lights! She turned then, to see if she could see anyone behind her.

Car lights swung into the alley and began to approach her. She threw her arm up to shield her eyes, at the same time shrinking back into some bushes.

The car, crunching on the gravel in the poorly maintained roadbed, crept past. When it had disappeared around the corner ahead, she tried to emerge, but felt herself held by a series of small arms that had stuck into her shirt, her shorts, and even into her hair. She had chosen a rose bush to shelter in.

She recognized the bush, in the alley behind her house. Her mother had loved the leggy bush, with pale pink roses that bloomed ten months out of the year. But now, she was held tight in its embrace. Listening for her pursuer, she untangled herself and slipped into the darkened yard.

She crept to the hose that she knew lay coiled in the corner of the patio. Cautiously, she turned it on. Soon, a trickle of water gushed over her feet. She wiped the nozzle and then brought it to her mouth. The first gulps were soothing on her throat. Then, she tasted the metallic, cold, almost sweetness of the water out of a hose. They had always drunk from a hose as kids, thinking it better than the inside tap. She was relieved not to have to go inside to slake her raging thirst.

A soft brush on her ankle caused her to utter an 'Eeeek." In her heightened state of anxiety, she had forgotten about her sweet kitty. She looked down to see the cat at her feet, asking for a pet and her dinner. Very cautiously checked the outside water bowl for the cat and whispered that dinner would be later. She then crept around the side of the house. She cowered in the bushes at the side of the house until she saw the lights of a car pull into her driveway.

She waited until she was sure of the car, then bent and tiptoed to the passenger side door. She softly opened it.

"Very, what's this all about?" Joey said. Then she looked at Very. "My god. What happened to you?"

"Some bad choices. But I have news. Drive to your house. I can't stay here. I dare not hang around my own house, not tonight." Very crawled into the car and pulled the seatbelt across her chest. "Drive, now, please Joey. There's a crazy bad guy out there and I'm running away."

They were silent on the drive until they turned down Joey's street. Very heaved a sigh of relief. No one had followed; she was safe now. As the garage door closed behind them, Very coughed out a short version of the events. Joey sat, her mouth open in astonishment. "You went down there alone? Why would you do that? And you didn't tell anyone where you were going? Even a text, even a quick phone message?"

"No phone connectivity. It was a mistake. But, I have news."

They went into the house, Very was pointed to the shower and some old clothes of Joey's that were clean, but a trifle tight. Joey sat with Very across her from as she plucked the rest of the cactus quills from Very's hands and put some disinfectant on the scrapes on her arms and legs. Very told more.

"He confessed. Curly, that is, Glenn Wilson, admitted that he had 'done away with' Danny Boy. And he threatened to kill me."

"How did you get him to confess? Really Very, that is incredible!" Joey said. "Oh, here is the man."

Joey jumped up and greeted her husband, resplendent in uniform, with a quick peck on his cheek.

"I've brought the reinforcements, as requested. I need to keep out of all of this. You understand, don't you, Very?" Officer Sanchez turned to Very.

"Yeah, I do." Very peeked over his shoulder to see two other officers waiting to talk with her.

Very repeated her story, more coherently this time, to the sheriff's representatives. They produced a map and Very tried to pinpoint the encampment where she had found Curly. She also tried to find the route she took up the bluffs.

One of the deputies laughed as Very described the cactus patch and the mad scramble up the steep slope. "That section is the one we use for rescue training. I know where that little patch of cactus is. Whoooo, that's one tough climb!"

The officials got on their radios and spoke with others in the field. They wandered outside and Very could hear the squeak and rumble of voices.

Joey made macaroni and cheese and salad. She made extra, knowing that some of the crew outside hadn't eaten. And she also knew, because Very had once confessed, that mac and cheese was her favorite meal as a child. The ultimate comfort food was what Joey was creating for Very. Very declined a glass of wine. The alcohol might make her shaky or in some way compromise her clarity. She needed to be clear-headed tonight.

"Did you really go down, or rather come up the hill, like straight up?" Joey asked, the second glass of wine she had going to her head. "The boys always wanted to do stupid things like that, but I never gave in. I guess they and their father did things like that when I wasn't with them. But you, Very! I know that you have done some wild things in your life, but this has got to rank up there with the most adventuresome. Or would you call it just stupid?"

"Ill-advised, thoughtless, reckless, rash, hot-headed. And yeah, maybe stupid. But I felt compelled. I've been beating my head against a wall for the past week or so. This seemed like the break I needed. And I needed to know. Of course, I haven't got all of it yet, but when Babe Harger died without telling anybody much, I felt so frustrated. I couldn't say anything like that to her daughter, not then, but the pieces were beginning to fit in. Now, we can begin to fit in the other ones."

Suddenly, there was a series of noises outside. Squawking radios, shouting, laughter, more radio noises.

Joey's husband came back inside. "They have him. Caught him in his lair, just where Very said it was." He turned to Very. "They found your backpack, which fits with your story. So that's a good sign. They are taking him to jail. Also, drugs and paraphernalia. And oh, they found a gun. You were one lucky lady. But he is in custody, so you are safe."

Very sank down on the sofa and tears of relief rolled down her face. It was the first reaction she had had besides fear in hours. She called a good neighbor to give her cat some food outside and let Joey lead her to a bed.

She fell asleep immediately, but woke up in terror three times. Her hands throbbed in pain. She stumbled through Joey's house trying to find a medicine cabinet with some aspirin or anything for the dull ache that was preventing her sleep. Finally, at 5:30, with soft new light coming through the blinds, she fell into an uneasy sleep, a short nap. But this time, she dreamt of a climb up the hillside that was swift and easy, almost like flying. When she arrived at the top, she peaked over the edge, wanting to see what was there, what the next chapter would be.

She woke, sunlight in her eyes.

Chapter Thirty: To the Jail

Very got up, tying an old bathrobe of Joey's around her for modesty's sake. She wandered into the kitchen and found Joey and her husband already drinking coffee. She helped herself. The sheriff's deputy had showered and shaved, but his eyes still drooped with lack of sleep.

Joey had the answer. "I'll drive you home and you can get into your own clothes. I think you need to visit the authorities again. I can drive you if you want."

"Thanks. I don't feel as bad as I should, surprisingly. I feel energized today. Now that I know who killed Danny Boy, I can rest easier. And knowing that he is locked up helps too. Ready when you are."

Very collected her filthy clothes from the day before and even declined to put on her dusty boots. She went barefoot to the car. As they pulled out of the driveway, they waved to Joey's husband, who was now getting ready to go to work.

"He looks really tired," Very commented to Joey. "I thought he was supposed to be out of all of this?"

"That's my sweetie. He has this insatiable desire to know, to be in on everything. He couldn't let it go. I don't know what time he came back last night, but it was really late. I need to try to get him to do more regular type exercise, and eat better. Cops and their donuts!"

Very stared out the window as they drove to her house, up on the hill. The day they had moved, her dad was so proud of himself. Finally, he had 'made it', moved into a classy neighborhood. Her mother was giggly with the idea of her own pool and a big yard for her flowers. The day promised to be another hot one; not a cloud in the sky, haze gathering over the city. But up there, in the hills, the breeze came up every afternoon, and it would be cooler than down in the flats.

As they drove south on Manor and took the tight turn onto Panorama, Very looked over at the bluffs. She couldn't see where she had been the day before, but she could see the long line of the bluffs, their dull yellow color slashed with dark shadows. She had climbed straight up one of those black knife cuts.

At her house, Very quickly found some clean clothes, fed the cat, grabbed a bite to eat and was back to the car within fifteen minutes.

Joey had been admiring the late blooming roses. "You have done such a great job with your mother's roses. They looked watered and fed and deadheaded and... loved!"

Very looked at the line of roses, now forty years old and in need of replacement. "Believe me, it was not a labor of love. It was guilt that made me do it. But yeah, they do look nice. I hadn't noticed."

"To the jail." Joey had spoken with her husband and it had been decided that Very would help in their interview with Curly. "You know that it's downtown, don't you, not out in Oildale?"

"Oh, I hadn't realized. Not that I have need for such knowledge, in normal times." Very put on her sunglasses against the morning glare and they were off.

When they arrived, Joey cautioned Very from bringing anything but the most essential of ID into the jail. "The building is secure and everyone is searched. They will let me in with you, but you can't take anything in with you. Hardly anything."

Joey led the way to the small visitor's section of the jail. As promised, they were searched and then they took seats in the small waiting room. No one else was here, as it was still too early for business. They settled in to wait.

Suddenly, the door opened, and Father Sullivan walked in, wearing his black suit with a dog collar. He immediately spied Very and approached her, both his hands held out to her. "Oh, what news! What terrible events!"

"Oh my god! Yes, I was terrified. It took me hours to calm down. I'm just here to make sure that he's interrogated properly, asked the right questions. Just to make sure it all comes out. I want everything that's been hidden for all these years to be exposed. All the details. Everything!"

"Yes, we will make sure of that. I promise. We need closure on this one. Of course…" Father Sullivan turned as the door in the back opened.

"Killer," said the uniformed man. "Good to see you!" He thrust out his hand and Father Sullivan shook it enthusiastically.

"Killer?" Very said. "Really?" The hairs on the back of her neck prickled.

"Oh no, just a stupid nickname from my days playing football. You know, when you've been saddled with a name like Clarence, you need something else. Pay no attention, he's just one of the guys from way back."

Father Sullivan turned back to the matter at hand. "We will make sure that it is done properly. Of course, he basically confessed to me, but if this is done the right way, no one will be able to say that I broke any vows of the confessional."

"Wow, he confessed to you too? Then that's it. It's true. And we can make sure it all comes out." Very said, relief washing over her face.

"You met him? You talked with him? What did he say to you? When was this?" Father Sullivan seemed surprised to hear this news from Very.

"Oh, I thought you knew all about it! I was chased up the bluffs. He ran after me, shouting that he would kill me. Thank goodness, I didn't know he had a gun. The crazy man threatening me was bad enough. Oh yeah, I had quite an evening."

"When exactly was this? What time?" Father Sullivan looked puzzled.

"Sunset. Or thereabouts. I wasn't quite sure of the exact time. But the sun had just gone down."

"At the bluffs? At sunset? Are you sure about the time?"

"Yeah, of course I'm sure. Why are you asking?"

"Because it couldn't have been. He was sitting right in front of me. Confessing. Details. He thought it was all going to be covered up. You know, confessing to a priest, sacred confessional and all."

"I don't understand. What made him confess? I mean, the way he said it, the words he used, that wasn't a confession with details. Not like what it seems he told you." Very said.

"He was quite specific."

"I thought he was on drugs, the eyes and the movements. And so, when he told me, it was as if he had made some sort of mistake by telling me. Like he wasn't able to control himself, watch what his tongue was saying. I think he said things that he later regretted."

"Hmmm. I don't know about that."

"When they told me that they had caught him, I didn't realize that he had talked to you. I thought they had gone to the camp, down by the bluffs, where I found him. But I guess that was later."

"Camp? Down by the bluffs? No, he was in the Homeless Shelter."

Very and Father Sullivan looked at each other; question marks biting into their faces.

"Who are we talking about?" Very asked.

Father Sullivan looked at Very and Very looked at Father Sullivan.

"Curly."

"Q-Ball."

Very spoke first. "You told me he was there, so I went there to find him."

"But that was Curly. You found him? And he confessed? He said that he had murdered Danny Harger?"

Very hesitated and then said, "No, he didn't say, 'I murdered Danny Boy.' But he implied that he had. He very strongly implied that he had made sure Danny wouldn't be around anymore. It was as close a confession as I think you can get without uttering the exact words. But then I told him that Danny Harger had been found, in the orchard. He didn't know that. And then he realized that he had confessed and he attacked me. I ran. But what is this about Q-Ball?

"I went looking for him since I knew that he often went to a particular shelter. They knew him there and if he was sober, they would let him in. Then, when I got there, I found a private space and had a chat with him. He'd heard about Danny Boy. I told you, he thought that it would be covered by rules of confession, and so he admitted he had done it. He thought I wasn't going to tell anyone."

"So, do you think they were in it together? They both had something to do with Danny's murder?"

"That's what it looks like. Wow. That is some secret to keep. How can you trust someone with a secret like that? And they went on with their lives. They had a duo, a band, that was moderately successful. And they both had careers, if you could call it that, as drug dealers and petty thieves." Father Sullivan paused in thought.

"If Q-Ball knew about finding Danny, why didn't he tell Curly? Surely, that was something they both needed to deal with. I mean, eventually, the investigation would have found out something, and it would lead back to those two. Wouldn't it?"

The same uniform that had greeted Father Sullivan earlier reappeared. He wore a look that could be interpreted as surprise, fear, incredulity, astonishment and a soupçon of disbelief.

Both Very and Father Sullivan turned to him.

Father Sullivan asked, "What's the matter?"

"They're gone, both of them."

"They escaped? How can that be possible? Weren't they locked up? I thought that no one would have any bail until today. What happened?" Father Sullivan asked.

"No, not escaped, dead."

For five seconds there was silence as this information worked its way into the consciousness of those in the room.

"Dead? Two men dead?"

"Well, they were locked up together," the uniform started to explain. "We all thought that was a pretty good joke, or maybe not. You see, we knew they knew each other. And there was information that we thought might be exchanged, like talking. Maybe getting their alibis straight or something. They could at least catch up with each other, if nothing else. And, there was a guard there. Kinda out of sight, you see. Just listening, but not strictly legal, I guess. But we had no idea anything could go wrong. And then the guard got sick and left his post. It wasn't his fault. Canteen food, bad hamburger he said. Anyway, he let someone know he was gone, and I guess they decided it was okay, or they didn't have anyone else. Oh, heads will roll over this."

"Or maybe not," Father Sullivan said. "An honest mistake? Will we ever know? But what happened? You said they were both dead? Murder? Suicide?"

The uniform chose his words carefully, "Not for the press, you understand, but it looks like they had a fight. Heads banged against the wall, hands on throats. God, a mess. Blood and…" He looked at Very and left the rest of his description hanging.

"This is so bizarre as to be unbelievable." Father Sullivan looked at Very.

"Where does this go from here?" Very asked. "We had confessions, or as good as. At least we know they were involved in Danny Harger's death. But now, they are both dead. Two dead men. No case. Nowhere to take this."

Father Sullivan sank onto a hard bench and put his head in his hands. "Where to go, what to do? This is impossible."

The uniform spoke up, "Well, you know what they say, 'Truth is stranger than fiction.'"

Chapter Thirty-one: Where is Frankie Monroe

After returning from the jail, Very retreated to Joey's backyard with a cup of coffee. Joey left her alone for a time, waiting for calmness to return to her friend. Then she joined her on the peaceful patio. The birds chirruped, the breeze played with the branches of the tall trees; peace descended on all who sat there.

Very sighed. "I guess it is safe to go home. My pursuer is dead. He killed Danny Boy, along with Q-Ball. I guess we can say the same of poor Q-Ball, he killed Danny Harger and Curly. Now they both have earned their just desserts. But I'm not satisfied. I want to know what happened in that jail cell. And what happened before it. Father Sullivan told me that Q-Ball confessed to him, but that it was under doubtful circumstances."

"Yeah," Joey added. "I heard, not for casual consumption, you understand? I heard that Q-Ball, Stan Leon, had declined to make a statement. So, no confession there. You know they picked him up on a violation of probation. Being on probation is totally miserable for someone like him. You're not allowed to do anything suspicious, so it's really easy to find a reason to haul you to jail. He probably would have gotten bail soon. But…"

"What do you think? Murdered each other? Decided to commit suicide together? No, no, don't tell me anything. They're both gone. That's the end of them and they can't tell me anything beyond the grave." Very sunk her head onto her chest, a thick knot between her eyebrows. "Unsatisfactory."

"What is your next step? Will you keep looking for Frankie?"

"Babe Harger is dead too. Father Sullivan, who ran with that crowd, says he never met Frankie. I haven't exhausted all the leads, but I'm getting close. I went into this search with one dead body. Now there are three more! And they all went to their graves knowing things they wouldn't tell me."

"But you knew, going into this, that it was always a long shot. That 37 years was a long time, with no trail, no news, no nothing. You have to at least entertain the idea that Frankie is dead too." Joey leaned forward, trying to catch Very's eye. "What did you really expect to find?"

Very's phone rang. She pulled it out of her purse and looked at the name. She lifted her hand in a gesture of, 'let me get this' to Joey and stood.

"Yeah, hi, Cassandra. I can call you that, can't I? Listen, I don't want to bother you too much at this time in your life. I know that things are moving fast…"

Very paused to listen. "Well, there are some people you might want to meet, if you have time. This afternoon? How about four o'clock? Here's the address." Very dictated an address. "I'll meet you there. Yeah, bye."

Joey looked askance at Very. "So, are you finished with the PI?"

"Oh, no. I still haven't looked everywhere for Frankie. There are many other databases to go. And besides, he kinda, sorta, said I had a job, if I wanted it. I'll think about that. Could use some money until my Social Security checks kick in and it might be fun, something to do. Just part-time, when I want to. I can't spend all my time sorting my mom's junk."

"Okay, if you are ready, I'll take you home now. Or do you want some more coffee?"

"Home, to my cat. Hmmm. Home. My home?" Very got up and reluctantly left the peacefulness of the patio.

As Joey pulled into the driveway at 'her' home, Very looked at it again. She had lived here, mostly, since she was twelve years old. It was 'her' house and now. She looked at it again, with the eyes of a new owner. What did she see?

It wasn't her home. It was her mother's. Her mother had planted those rose bushes, these trees. She had had a good eye for color and creating a 'wild yet domestic' look. She had chosen the color to have it painted and when Very suggested the blue on the shutters should be a more vibrant hue, her mother overruled her, saying, "It's my house, I'll paint it whatever colors I want." Very had contributed nothing to the upkeep of the house, other than years of labor in the garden and the kitchen and the pool and the cleaning... But her mom had paid the bills, the mortgage, the taxes, the insurance. It wasn't Very's house and it wasn't her style.

Now it was in her name as well. But did she want to continue living here, in this neighborhood? The house needed work, and new windows, maybe solar panels. Solar was becoming the wave of the future; shouldn't she join that wave? And the pool needed renovations. And what about a heater, so Very could swim into the fall, and earlier in the spring?

As soon as she entered the house, she saw the clutter, the shelves overflowing, the cupboards full of dishes. Her mother's bedroom contained boxes and heaps of clothes and stuff, piles and piles of stuff.

She fed the cat some treats, brushed her and then went in search of a pencil and paper. She would make a list. In order, all the things she needed to do.

By three, she had a list, had created a series of boxes, labeled them, and placed them strategically to be loaded with the items going in them. Sissy had a couple of boxes, Goodwill had even more and there was one labeled 'trash.' She took a shower and dressed carefully, trying to choose something decent, not stained, torn or missing a button. She had become lazy since she had retired. She even put on some makeup and combed her hair carefully, wishing that she had had a haircut recently.

She drove to Sunny and Marty Monroe's house and parked in the shade on the opposite side of the street. She waited for Cassandra.

At four exactly, Cassandra drove up and parked in front of the house. She got out, and looked at a small piece of paper in her hand. Very got out of her car and greeted her. They approached the house and then Very noticed a box in Cassandra's hand. "A gift?"

"Food. Always a good thing to bring, isn't it? It's just a box of cookies, but I couldn't come empty-handed, could I?" Cassandra looked expectantly at the front door, wondering what lay beyond.

Very rang the doorbell and listened for the shuffle of feet. Then the door opened and Sunny pushed open the screen door to let the guests enter. "Marty, Very's here. And… someone else."

The two visitors walked into the gloomy interior. Sunny scrunched up her face and looked hard at the newcomer. Cassandra Harger held out the box of cookies. "I brought something," she said in her throaty voice.

Sunny had begun to stretch out her hand, but halted in mid-stretch. "Oh." She stepped closer and peered into Cassandra's face. "Oh, Marty, come and meet our guest."

Very stepped back and let the three women, three generations, meet. The thread that bound them together was missing. It was a very small gift that Very could give the Monroes.

"Hi, I'm Cassandra Harger. You can call me Cassandra, or Cassie, or Sandra, whatever you want. I answer to all sorts of names." Cassandra smiled at the Monroes, who continued to stare.

Marty was the first to break the spell. "You are, aren't you, Frankie's girl? His daughter?"

"What do you think, ladies, do we need DNA to tell us that?" Very asked the Monroes.

Cassandra sat down, uncomfortable at being scrutinized.

"No, she's Frankie all over again. Oh, that voice, smoky, husky, so charming." Sunny sat next to her on the couch and took Cassandra's hand. "And look at those eyes and that nose, and the hair. Just so similar, so much like him."

"My dad, Danny Harger, or who I thought was my dad, died before I was born, and so I never knew that I didn't look anything like him. I was nothing like my mother, but my dad was just a photo, I didn't know anything. When my mother was dying, she tried to tell me something about my father. Then, Very showed me the photo of Frankie. And I think I know that my mom was trying to tell me about Frankie. Frankie was my father, my biological father. It makes sense now."

"How did it happen? Before your folks were married?" Sunny asked.

"No, after. I was born more than a year after my parents were married. I checked the marriage certificate once. You know how kids are, snoopers. I just had no idea that my father wasn't my father. But when I saw the picture of Frankie, I could just feel it was the truth. And now, do we have anyway of proving it? I mean, I don't care that much, but… Is it possible to do a DNA test?"

Very explained quickly why neither of the Monroe women were in fact related to Frankie.

"You remember, Very, asking us if we had anything of Frankie's left? Well, technically that's not true. I have photos. Lots of pictures. I'll get them." Marty jumped up and went to the back of the house, returning within a minute with a photo album.

"Oh, and we need some iced tea to go with those cookies," Marty said.

Very rose and said, "I'll get it, you three talk."

When Very returned with a tray of glasses of iced tea and the cookies on a plate, the three women were looking at the photo album. Cassandra was asking questions about Frankie's hobbies and what he was good and bad at. She often said, "Oh, me too. I can't stand tuna fish sandwiches. Yucky, yucky. How weird is that?" And she laughed the throaty chuckle that Very remembered so well.

Very looked over Marty's shoulder at the photos as the reminiscences went on. At one point, Marty stood up and faced Very. "I really, really wish we could find something that had some DNA of Frankie's. He never gave you a lock of his hair?"

Very laughed. "He may have taken a snippet of mine, but he would never let me get near his gorgeous curls. No, I have nothing. Do you have anything besides these photos?"

Marty looked at a sideboard that held some more photos and shook her head. "You know," she said in a low voice, moving away from the two on the couch looking at the album. "I've thought a lot about Frankie in the last few days, ever since you came here, looking for anything to identify him. And I tried to think of anything he might have said in those last few months that might help us find him. And something did come up that I didn't understand at the time. But now that I see Cassandra, now maybe it makes sense.

"You see, one night I was staying up late, almost midnight, it must have been a Friday or Saturday night. It was around Halloween of that year, give or take a few days. I'm pretty sure it was before you met Frankie. Anyway, Frankie came in from wherever he had been, with his friends, I assumed. But he was being big brotherly, kind of giving me the 'wisdom' of his years. And he talked about being a good husband. And a good wife. He said that some of his friends wouldn't agree, but that he thought being a good husband and a good wife was being loyal and faithful. He seemed angry, a little, and maybe disappointed in himself, or a friend. It was not clear what brought it on. But he did say to me, "Be a good wife, be a loyal wife.

"And then when he met you and we met you and then, the baby and getting married, I was at first a little disappointed. I mean, don't take this the wrong way, Very, but you're not really glamorous or drop dead gorgeous or anything. And I was a little sad to not have a super beautiful sister-in-law. But when I saw how happy he was,

I was okay with it. I think I knew that he had found someone who would be a good wife, a loyal wife. Which is what he wanted. I think you would have been happy together in that way, loyal and faithful. Now, money problems and the booze, and those friends of his… That might have done the marriage in, but not the two of you.

"So, I'm thinking that he knew about unfaithful wives," said Marty, nodding her head in Cassandra's direction. "And maybe that's why, when he met you, he was going to make it right. He was going to be a good husband."

"Do you think he knew about Babe Harger's pregnancy? He must have done, he ran with that crowd. And he must have done something to make it happen," Very said.

"But just because the two of them had an affair, doesn't mean that the baby was his. I mean, she could have been sleeping with both of them at the same time and who was to know who was the father before the kid was born? And then, when she had the baby, both Danny and Frankie had disappeared. It didn't really matter at that point. Of course, as she grew up, Babe had to have known that Frankie was the father."

"What a woman, to have carried that secret for all those years. And that accident, maybe it wasn't truly an accident? Maybe there was something more to it?"

"Oh, Very," said Cassandra from the couch. "I am so glad you brought me here. I know that there have been so many things happening, but this is a happy time for me. I feel like I found something that was lost. Maybe I never knew that I had lost it, but there was a hole in my life. I think that I had always thought that it was because my dad died before I was born, and I didn't know him. But now, I think it was deeper than that. I can feel something extraordinary going on here. And these," she ran her hand over the childhood photos of Frankie and his sister Marty. "These are so precious. We're going to get copies, aren't we?"

"Of course," Marty said. "We might even have the negatives. Let's make a plan to get these copied and printed."

A half hour later, just after Cassandra and Very left the house, Very turned to Cassandra. "You never got to tell me exactly what your mother told you on the morning she died. Just that it was about your father. Do you think she was trying to tell you about Frankie?"

"Yes, I do. How do you tell your daughter something like that? It would have been a hard thing to do, and I think I understand why she kept it a secret all those years. Don't upset the applecart. I had a family, grandparents, cousins, and I never wanted for anything. I had a dad; his picture was on the shelf. So why say anything?"

"It's not fair to judge our parents too harshly. We did not live their lives."

"Yeah," Cassandra said. "Think of all the stupid, mean or cruel things we did. I'm not going to hold it against my mother. I had no idea what the circumstances were. I want to leave it at that. I'm glad I found Frankie's 'family'. Wow, what a collection we are."

"You know, you and I are related. My child would have been your half-brother or sister. That would have made you my... stepdaughter? How about that?" Very smiled at Cassandra and gave her a little hug.

"A lot of family!"

That evening, Very sat on the patio with her cat. The evening had fallen and she looked for stars. She saw stars as a kid, but now there was air pollution and light pollution. There were no more stars in Bakersfield.

A faint fog threatened to cloud her mind, but she breathed deeply and tried to calm herself. She could see them now, sitting in a row way in the back of the Nile Theater. The four of them. Babe sat on the end, next to her was Danny Boy, then Frankie and Very sat beside Frankie. She didn't pay attention to the other couple, she'd never met them, and she didn't realize that Frankie knew them. She thought it was just by chance. She remembered that Frankie spoke to the man, the one she knew now was Danny Boy Harger. The words would not come to her; she could not conjure up what was said that night so long ago.

She knew where Danny Boy was, and Babe. And she was here, watching the night sky. But where was Frankie Monroe?

About the Author

Phyllis Wachob has been a fan of mysteries since her childhood and an English teacher for over 30 years. While teaching and living in many countries around the world, including Japan, China, Taiwan, Singapore, Australia, Egypt and Turkey, she has visited over 75 countries. Inspired by her own and others' adventures as English teachers, she has chronicled her travels in a series of mysteries set in exotic places and interesting times. She still teaches English in Bakersfield, California, where she now resides. Her latest series, Kern Kapers Mysteries, is set in her hometown. For more information visit Phyllis' website at phylliswachob.com.

CPSIA information can be obtained
at www.ICGtesting.com
Printed in the USA
FSHW011300091220
76749FS